COTSWOLD

MOLES

Also by Michael Spicer

Final Act
Prime Minister Spy
Cotswold Manners
Cotswold Murders
Cotswold Mistress
A Treaty Too Far

Michael · Spicer

COTSWOLD

·|——————————————————|·

MOLES

St. Martin's Press   New York

All the characters in this book are fictitious; so too are most of the events.

Library of Congress Cataloging-in-Publication Data

Spicer, Michael.
       Cotswold moles / Michael Spicer.
          p.   cm.
       "A Thomas Dunne book."
       ISBN 0-312-09263-6 (hardcover)
       I. Title.
PR6069.P498C63   1993
823'.914—dc20   93-3525
                                             CIP

First edition: June 1993

10 9 8 7 6 5 4 3 2 1

To Ann, my wife and most valued critic, written in the twenty-fifth year of our marriage, with love

—Cropthorne, 1992

COTSWOLD

MOLES

1

A little to the left of the tiny, white-painted cricket pavilion, I could just make out the body of a man swinging from the branch of an old horse-chestnut tree. It was almost hidden in the shadows of the heavy foliage and had I not known what I was looking for, I probably would not have noticed it, certainly not from the road.

I climbed over some iron railings and began to run across the newly mown grass, wet and slippery from the overnight dew. To my right a ragged line of chimney-pots gently puffed smoke towards a ridge of the Cotswold hills, still partly shrouded in morning mist. Above me a hazy blue sky promised another warm spring day. About fifty metres across the green I stumbled on a molehill. Recovering my balance, I even managed to increase my pace. Thankfully I was wearing a pair of old jeans. A skirt would have slowed me down and I knew that I did not have much time. The police would be here any minute.

Despite the high state of my physical fitness, I was slightly out of breath when I reached the chestnut tree. I stood for a moment looking up into its thick branches and inhaling gulps of damp moss-tasting air. The deep-puce flowers of the tree were like splashes of blood on the spring leaves. Then, with deliberate slowness, taking in every detail, I began to lower my eyes to the place where the corpse hung suspended, with its feet about a metre above the ground.

The body was of an elderly man whom I knew to have been in his late sixties. Its round bald head had rolled forward, presumably closing the eyelids as it did so. The upper lip was badly swollen and the cheeks had decompressed, pulling the jaw backwards and leaving the mouth to form itself into a black circular hole, around which two flies were buzzing angrily at each other. The rope around the neck had been tied at one end to a short branch and then tossed a metre and a half higher to where the trunk of the tree divided to form a suitable cleft. The cord was white and surprisingly thin, like the painter of a small boat.

From the clothes he was wearing, the man might well have been a sailor (though, as far as I knew, this was not actually the case). A pair of muddied trousers was suspended from his stomach and a thick polo-necked sweater covered the torso. One of his rubber boots had fallen to the ground and lay on its side next to an overturned stool whose aluminium legs and torn black pseudo-leather seat brought back to me memories of waiting for contacts in seedy Soho bars.

I paused for a moment. I had dealt many times before with corpses such as this one, but to do so again still required me consciously to draw on all my training and experience.

In the far distance, a blue light began to blink from the main road. It began slowly to zigzag up the hill towards the village. I had to act now.

I reached up towards the left leg. A thick brown woollen sock had slipped half-way down the calf, uncovering a patch of pure white skin. I grasped the ankle with one hand and swung the body onto a slant. The piece of paper I was looking for had been rolled into the shape of a cigar and was now protruding downwards from the pocket. I stretched my right arm towards it, but it was just beyond my reach. This was one of those occasions when my petiteness was a real handicap. I gave the leg a shake. The little roll of paper loosened itself from the opening of the pocket and fell in a direct line to the ground.

I knelt down and unrolled the paper on a pile of dead leaves. Its message was surprisingly short. Written in pencil and with uneven capital letters, it said simply, 'I am responsible for Mrs Langhorn's death. Now that she is gone I know that I cannot live without her.' There was no signature.

I refolded the note just as a white car drew up at the gate on the far side of the cricket pitch. The light on its roof was still flashing as a lone uniformed policeman stepped out from it onto the narrow country road. He was a tall man who was evidently finding some difficulty in unbending himself from the cramped inside of his vehicle. He adjusted his peaked cap and seemed to peer over in my direction. His round rustic face looked startled when he spotted me.

'What the hell are you doing?' he shouted. The wind must have been behind him because I had no difficulty in making out his ponderous Gloucestershire accent, even though he must have been some hundred metres away from me.

I decided I had better go over and talk to him. I folded the little piece of paper and began walking across the field. About twenty metres away the policeman stood firmly with legs apart and hands on hips on the other side of the railings, like a male washerwoman. When I reached the railings I pulled out a piece of plastic, suspended on a small chain around my neck, from its resting place above my bosom and pointed its face in his direction.

'Jane Hildreth,' I said, 'from London.'

He looked down at me with that very special air of distaste which members of the local constabulary reserve for interloping opposite numbers from the world outside, especially from the metropolis.

'So you're the Lady Hildreth that's come along to poke around at the Manor. I would have thought that our force would have been quite capable of dealing with the Langhorn business on its own. What a waste of taxpayers' money, all you people streaming down from London, just because a rich lady died without leaving any heirs.'

'There have been others from London?'

'There will be. I'm prepared to bet on it. It's bloody ridiculous. We may be the smallest force in the country, but we've got a better solve rate than the rest of you put together, and that includes murder.'

'You think she may have been murdered?'

'I didn't say that. In fact, I thought I was rather suggesting the opposite, a natural death, nothing for a sensible policeman to worry about.'

There was a whiny, mechanical tone to his voice. Whether he admitted it or not, the emphasis on 'murder' had been real enough. He had pronounced it with no obvious ring of excitement, more with a certain dolefulness which I took to signal his concern that this could mean hard work and a lot of aggro from the office. He stood for a moment, staring downwards in silent thought. Then, as if suddenly recollecting what it was that had brought us together, he looked up at me, his suspicion rising to a new peak.

'What were you doing to Jack Swinton's body just now?'

'I wasn't engaging in any mystical rites, I assure you, Constable.'

'You shouldn't have tampered with the body without permission. My orders are very clear on that: no one near the body until our CID get here, and when I said *our* CID, that's what I meant.'

'Did you know him?' I asked.

'Jack Swinton? Of course I did. In a sort of a way Jack was a bit of a mate of mine. I cannot for the life of me imagine why he did himself in. He was a steady sort of bloke, was Jack, very steady.'

He seemed to relax a little. His manner was becoming almost confidential.

'Perhaps he didn't.'

'Didn't what?'

'Do himself in.'

'You think he was murdered?'

'I have no idea.'

He changed the subject and some of his former coldness returned.

'It was you that telephoned us from the Manor, wasn't it?'

'Yes.' I wondered for a moment what idyllic rhythm of life I had broken for him by my call. Mornings of checking gun licenses around the farms, followed by a pub lunch fraternizing with the locals? An afternoon visit to the vicar to discuss the Flymo missing from the churchyard? A cup of tea with gypsies, interrupted perhaps by a call on the car radio ordering him to report to a local big house where the faulty burglar alarm had gone off again? Murder and/or suicide by hanging belonged for him to another world. It was what no doubt he had left the big city to escape from, together with the late-night gang fights by the central bus stop, the race riots and the Saturday football mobs. Presumably he accepted that what he was doing wasn't modern police work. It wouldn't earn him promotion; he would never wear a sergeant's stripes. But he probably got free fishing out of it; and the country girls were uncomplicated, not like this little blonde bombshell from London with the posh accent, the designer jeans and the leather boots and, okay, the sexy looks. I was not his type, not his type at all. My imagination had run ahead further than was necessary. I looked past him down the road.

'I imagine someone else is going to arrive soon to help you?' I asked. His shoulders slumped and his lower lip curled forwards. He looked rather crest-fallen; he seemed to feel that I had passed an unfair judgement on his competence.

'The ambulance should be here in a few minutes,' he conceded grudgingly. 'Headquarters say that the CID should arrive from Gloucester in half an hour or so.'

'In the meantime, you will guard the body?'

'Too true. He's not to be moved until they get here, not even by important people from London.' He looked directly at me to make sure he had scored a bulls-eye.

I handed him the suicide note.

'This should cheer you up,' I said. 'I wonder if you would mind giving it to the CID when they finally make it. I'm sure they'll check its authenticity. If they want to chat, I'll be up at the Manor.'

I began to climb over the railings. His thick eye-brows folded together as he focused his full powers of concentration on the message from the dead man. His slightly bloodshot, unintelligent eyes moved slowly backwards and forwards several times across the paper. When at last he spoke, it was without any hint of a prurient undertone.

'Jack Swinton worked for Mrs Langhorn for over forty years. There was talk in the village that after Mr Langhorn passed away in the mid-1960s, he acted as her husband, if you know what I mean.' This coyness was his most endearing display of character yet.

'Do you think that Mrs Langhorn and Mr Swinton were lovers?' I asked.

He scratched the back of his neck and shifted his not inconsiderable weight from one leg to the other. For a moment he said nothing. Although embarrassed by it, he was evidently taking the question seriously. When he spoke, the words came out in something of a rush.

'Frankly, no. Not at least in the last ten years or so. She was too far gone by then. I don't mean physically, mind. They say she was as strong as an ox right to the end. I mean here.' He pointed the forefinger of his right hand to his forehead.

'You are saying she was mad?'

'I know darned well she was,' he replied with a new assurance.

'That's interesting,' I said. 'Interesting, that is, that you should be so sure. After all, she hadn't been seen in public for fifteen years.'

'After you've been in a post as long as I've been in this one, you get to know about these things.' The questioning of his judgement had, I suppose quite understandably, brought on a new bout of defensiveness.

'I suppose you knew a lot of the people who worked for her.' I hoped I sounded gentler.

'And that was easier said than done,' he replied.

'How come?'

'Except for young Jack over there, they never stayed with her for more than a few months. Too much abuse and not enough pay, that's what they all said, except for Jack.'

His eyes wandered past me and attempted to focus on the cadaver swinging in the shadows of the distant tree.

'I hope they come soon.' He seemed to be speaking to himself when he added, 'They told me to keep him exactly as he was when I found him, but I can't go on leaving Jack swinging there like that. In a few minutes I'm going to have him down, whatever they say. It's a wonder the word hasn't got around the village yet.'

'He can't be seen from the road,' I said, 'not unless someone has pointed him out to you. As I told your people when I rang the station, I doubt if anyone had been in the house before I arrived this morning, so I imagine I am the only person to have seen the words he scrawled in chalk on the kitchen table.'

'Saying he had gone to hang himself by the pavilion.' The dead-pan way in which this was spoken gave a somewhat surreal twist to our conversation.

'What sort of a man was Jack?' I asked.

'What do you mean?'

'My guess is that we will have to know a little more about him before we can be sure how he died. From what I saw of the body, I don't think you can take it for granted that he hanged himself. He could just as easily have been murdered.'

'And the message in the kitchen?'

'It could have been written for him.'

The policeman hesitated and then said somewhat obscurely, 'I knew him most of my life but, there again, I didn't know him at all, if you know what I mean.' I wasn't sure that I did.

'Where used you to meet him?'

'In the Black Horse over there at the top of the hill. I drop in most evenings,' he added hurriedly, 'when I come off duty, that is. Jack would come in there about twice a week.'

'Any idea what he did on the other nights?'

He shrugged. 'Looked after the old lady, I should imagine.'

There was the wail of a siren from the direction of the main road. I adjusted the lapel of my suede jacket.

'The ambulance seems to have got here rather quicker than you expected,' I said.

The policeman didn't seem to hear me. His mind evidently was tuned to cope with one issue at a time.

'When I think of it, I didn't know him at all well.

None of us did. I'll tell you one thing, though, he wasn't as daft as he made out. Just occasionally, he would let slip and come out with something quite out of character. I remember when that Falklands War was on, he once said that he knew that the Argies had biological weapons. He said it with such authority that it made me wonder at the time whether he had some sort of inside information. Most of the time he was just like the rest of us country folk. You could have a bit of a laugh with him, but there again, he wasn't . . .' His voice trailed to a halt.

'Wasn't what?'

'Like the other blokes in the village.'

'In what way was he different?'

'When we used to tell dirty jokes, he didn't really join in. He was not really one of us. Perhaps he was too tied up with the lady.'

'Did she ever come into the pub?'

'Who? Mrs Langhorn? You must be joking. She never came into the village, let alone the pub. As you know, in recent years she didn't even leave her house. Jack did all the fetching and carrying that needed to be done.'

'Was he born in the village?' I asked.

He shook his head. 'No. That I do know. But I never did find out where he was from. I believe he came here much the same time as the Langhorns. He may even have come with them, for all I know.'

Behind him, the ambulance was passing the row

of old almshouses at the entrance to the village. Its siren had been turned off, but its blue light was still flashing.

'Time I moved on,' I said to the policeman. 'You know where to find me. In any case, I shall keep in touch with our Special Branch people in Gloucester.'

'Since when has Special Branch been in on murder inquiries?' he asked.

'Depends on what sort of murder it is,' I said. 'They like to come in if national security is involved. So does my department, for that matter.'

'And what department exactly would that be?' he asked.

'Box 500, better known as MI5.'

I left him scratching his head with the finger of one hand and fumbling inside his tunic for his two-way radio with the other.

2

Passing the tiny rectangular Norman church, I began to climb the road towards the war memorial. Here I turned left and made my way down a narrow muddy lane. A few hundred metres farther on, a pair of tall wrought-iron gates opened onto a gravel drive.

Studwell Manor is built very precisely as a square. A large part of its beauty lies in its symmetry. Although not particularly grand as manors in the Cotswolds go, it is an exquisite example of the very best of country Georgian architecture. It is flanked on three sides by lawns, behind which rise the rich green slopes of the hills. On the ground floor the long, elegant windows—that is, the ones that face south—have panoramic views of the open arable land below. Inside, undoubtedly the most important feature is the circular staircase with its stone steps and intricately carved wooden banisters. The quality of this craftsmanship continues throughout the four or five main bedrooms, whose ceilings and walls are covered with some of the most detailed wooden carving I have ever seen.

Devoted though I am to lovely architecture, I had not on this occasion come to admire the beauty of the house. I was much more concerned at that moment with the state of its contents. The chaos I had discovered when I had arrived earlier that morning is hard to describe. The house had clearly belonged to someone very rich. I had no doubt at all that many items lying around inside would fetch high prices at Christie's or Sotheby's, or wherever the Treasury Solicitor chose to have them auctioned. In the condition in which I had found them, however, they were forlorn and pathetic. Oil paintings by old masters were stacked in untidy heaps around the house. Leather-bound books were scattered about the hall and drawing-room. Mahogany antique furniture had been upended and crammed into every corner. Upstairs, open shoe cases had spewed their contents across beds and even into one of the baths. Hat boxes with Harrods labels were piled on top of each other like grown-up Legos. In several rooms the way was obstructed by mounds of expensive furs.

The scene had been unnatural. An act of vandalism or violence or burglary might have explained it, but somehow I did not feel that any of them were likely to be part of the story. In a strange way, there was a feeling almost of permanence about the mess. Certainly I felt it had been in there for some considerable period of time.

For the second time that day I paused under the mock Tudor arch. On this occasion I turned the key in the heavy front door. When I had approached the house earlier on, the door had been wide open. My surprise at this had slightly abated after I had found Jack Swinton's message. Evidently when the wretched fellow had slipped out into the night, he had had more pressing things on his mind than remembering to lock the front door behind him. In any event, before setting off in search of his body, I had made sure to locate a set of front-door keys, which, as it happened, had been hanging from a hook on the dresser in the kitchen.

Now that I was back in the house I was determined not to be further distracted. It was already clear that the task I had been sent to perform was not going to be an easy one. As a matter of fact, it was still not absolutely clear to me how I was going to carry out the instructions I had been given.

'Instructions' is probably too strong a word for the authority I was acting on. The more I thought about it, the flimsier it appeared to me was the pretext on which, uninvited, I had entered the property. My orders had been given to me in a manner which was unusual even by the standards of the organization I worked for. My boss had simply telephoned me the previous evening at my cottage in Chipping Campden. He had begun by asking me a question, itself a rare event. The chief didn't usually interrogate his agents, especially over the phone. If he phoned personally, which was not very often, it was typically with a crisp command. Any background chat was on a strictly need-to-know basis. On this occasion, he had begun very informally. His voice had sounded almost relaxed.

'Jane, did you ever come across a Mrs Langhorn?'

'I can't say the name rings any immediate bell, chief.'

'She used to live in your part of the world: Studwell Manor. That's near you, isn't it?'

I had to consider the point for a moment before answering.

'Yes, if I've got the right place, from where I live it's on the other side of Moreton-in-Marsh, about ten miles from here on the Stow road.'

'Mrs Langhorn died there last night.'

'And the department has an interest in her death?'

'I'm not sure' had been the unusually hesitant response. Decisiveness was normally one of the chief's strong suits. Under his leadership, the department very rarely wobbled about on the issue of when to intervene in a problem. Usually he was very clear about where the boundaries of the department's responsibilities lay. Certainly, once he had made up his mind to unleash his forces, the niceties of interdepartmental rivalry did not seem to trouble him unduly.

'I would be most grateful,' my boss had continued with what, quite astonishingly, had been a note of supplication, 'if you would be good enough to spend some of your weekend nosing around at the Manor. I've squared it with the local police. They are quite happy for you to go through the contents of the house. It's all a bit chaotic over there, I'm told.'

'I've squared it with the police.' That was odd in itself. The chief did not normally engage himself personally with such details. In retrospect I should have registered this as a signal of the importance he attached to the matter. Instead I had made a mild protest.

'Can't it wait until Monday?' My irritation had been genuine. I had promised to have Sunday lunch with my seventy-odd-year old friend and bodyguard, the Honourable Patricia Huntington. It had even been agreed between us that for once I would do the cooking. I had, in fact, been on the point of making a final decision to roast a leg of lamb with tarragon. Pat, I knew, would be particularly disappointed if these arrangements were to be cancelled. It was not the food she would miss; she had always been a modest eater, although a surprisingly good cook. It was the conversation. At her insistence, I had agreed to spend at least part of our time together plotting her return to active duty as a front-line agent with the service. I knew that she had been brushing up on her small-arms marksmanship for the occasion. Pat Huntington was not going to be a happy lady if our get-together was called off.

'I'm afraid not,' I had heard the chief say. 'On Monday morning the Treasury Solicitor's people will start clearing away her effects. I simply don't have enough information to ask them to delay their work.'

'Why the Treasury Solicitor?' I had asked.

'Mrs Langhorn had no known heirs. What's more, she left no will or final testament, so unless a blood relation steps forward pretty smartly and can prove his inheritance rights, her very considerable fortune will pass over to the state. It should go some way to helping with your and my pension.'

'Presumably the police have a guard on the house?' I had asked.

'The village bobby has been told to keep an eye on the place. Apparently there's an old retainer who lives in; I think he's called Swinton. He's been there for years. We have the impression, as a matter of fact, that, other than the old lady herself, Swinton has been the only permanent occupant for some time.'

'I'm surprised the local police aren't more involved,' I had persisted.

'Why should they be? From their point of view, there was nothing peculiar about Mrs Langhorn's death. She was, after all, in her eighties.'

'But we think otherwise.'

'I'm not sure' had been his unsatisfactory reply. 'But I will tell you that Mossad think otherwise. They believe she had all sorts of unsavoury foreign connections which should interest us.'

So that was it. Our old friends in Tel Aviv had put their oar in again. I wondered momentarily what would be the reaction of our political masters if they

found out how much traffic there was between ourselves and Mossad. Sometimes we practically lived in
each other's offices.

'And my job is to find out whether they're right?'
I asked.

'Exactly.'

'And if I knock on the front door and wave my
ID card at him, Mr Swinton will let me in?'

'Hopefully.'

'And if he doesn't, I go in anyway?'

'Precisely.'

3

I stood for a moment in the hall. Everything was as it had been on my first visit to Studwell Manor. Mrs Langhorn must have been a very odd person indeed to have left it in this state. I felt a twinge of sympathy for the people who would be coming the next day from the Treasury Solicitor's office. It was bad enough for them to have the job of clearing it all up; to record and value every item of it, as presumably they would have to do, was going to be a massive undertaking.

Thankfully, my task was more restricted. The first thing I would do was to collect whatever written evidence there was of Mrs Langhorn's contacts overseas. I began the search in the obvious places: drawers of desks, cabinets, dressing-tables, chests, boxes. I worked for two hours without stopping. At the end of this time I had failed to discover a single relevant document. More to the point, perhaps, I had found nothing to prove conclusively that Mrs Langhorn had existed at all. The absence of any photographs was particularly remarkable.

I sat down on the corner of a white silk quilted bedcover and looked at my watch: twelve-fifteen. I decided to take a break. I had promised to meet Pat Huntington for a bar snack in the pub up the road; it had been the best substitute we could arrange for the cancelled Sunday roast. I would have to launch a more detailed and widespread search after lunch, possibly with Pat's help.

I left the house by the back door. Turning left on a gravel path, I began to circle the building towards the main drive. The mist had completely cleared and the sun beat down pleasurably onto the back of my neck. Over to my right, half hidden by a ragged privet hedge, the shell of a swimming pool lay drained and covered in leaves. Someone had recently mown the lawns, but the several flower-beds were a tangled mass of weeds and dead vegetation. A flock of sheep began to bleat dolefully from somewhere out of sight in the hills behind me.

At the front of the house I headed straight down the drive to the main gates and out into the road. I glanced quickly to my right in the direction of the cricket ground. A small crowd of villagers, mainly children, stood in what seemed mesmerized silence around three police cars. The ambulance had left, presumably now well on its way to delivering Jack Swinton's remains to the mortuary in Gloucester.

I hurried in the opposite direction up the hill to

where I had left my white Mercedes sports car outside the Black Horse pub. As I reached it, I noted that Pat Huntington's 1950s Daimler was parked on the opposite side of the street. The Daimler had been a recent addition to her collection of seven vintage cars. When Pat had sounded out my views on her latest acquisition, I had made the mistake of questioning the practicality of a person of her age driving something so cumbersome around the Cotswold lanes. At the time of this conversation, Pat had been lying flat on her back beneath the car under debate, hammering noisily on some metallic part of its insides. I had not therefore been able to gauge her immediate reactions to my well-meant words of caution. On reflection, I have never received a proper response to them, for when she had finally emerged from the underbelly of the car, her nose and forehead smudged with oil, she had rather stiffly changed the subject.

I entered the Black Horse down two steps and through a creaky oak door. On the far side of the saloon bar a large log fire raged rather wastefully, given the outside temperature. Pat Huntington, evidently the only customer, sat next to the fireplace holding a large gin and tonic. She was dressed in brown corduroy trousers and a dark-blue denim shirt. Her aristocratic good looks glowed in the light of the fire. A curl of white hair fell to cover her forehead. A bit on the thin side perhaps these days, but certainly not bony, she was still a very attractive woman. Her eyes sparkled with enthusiasm as she spotted me.

'I suppose you know all about Mr Swinton who hanged himself last night by the cricket pavilion?' she opened enthusiastically.

'Mysterious deaths are matters for the police,' I said warily. 'My department's responsibilities are on the whole limited to matters of national security. So I have tried not to become too involved in the death of poor Mr Jack Swinton.'

No doubt I was smiling as I spoke. We knew each other too well for me to believe that she would take my words at their face value. She smiled and raised one of her distinguished-looking eyebrows. 'But it all ties in, doesn't it? He was apparently in cracking form when he came in last night for his usual four pints of ale.'

'Swinton was in here last night?'

'In this very room.'

I sighed. 'You've been talking to the staff, Pat. I thought the idea was to have a quiet off-duty Sunday pub lunch together: no business, just relaxation.'

She made a small gesture with her head towards the bar counter on the other side of the room. Standing behind it was a large man, probably in his sixties. His face was almost hidden between two thick white whiskers.

'He looks like something out of Dickens,' I whispered. 'I could have sworn he was in a play on TV last night.'

'He's full of jolly good information, that's what he is.' She waved an arm at him.

'A Campari and soda for my friend, please, and what is there to eat?' Her call was firm but cheery and polite.

His response was just as friendly.

'Be with you in a jiffy, my dear.'

Turning round, she giggled girlishly. She really did have a very pretty face. She suddenly addressed me in a conspiratorial half-whisper. 'It seems Mr Swinton was particularly expansive two nights ago about the last few days of Mrs Langhorn's life. Two days before she died she had a visitor. This was apparently a very rare occurrence. A dark-haired lady with what Mr Swinton called olive-coloured skin spent two hours with her. When she left, Mrs Langhorn was in tears. Afterwards she practically lived on the phone to her bank in Switzerland where, according to Bill Tomlinson, she kept most of her wealth in gold bars.'

'Bill Tomlinson?'

'Mine host over there.'

'Ah.' One of Pat's many qualities was the rapidity with which she learnt people's names and the length of time over which she remembered them.

'The missus will do you scampi and chips if you would like it,' he called from the bar. 'Otherwise it's sandwiches.'

'What sort?' Pat inquired.

'Cheese and onion, cheese and tomato, or just cheese,' he said.

'Just cheese for me,' I said.

'And one scampi and chips,' Pat added. 'I've had

a heavy morning on the cars and I'm ravenous.' I was delighted to hear that her appetite had returned. She definitely needed to put on a bit of weight. A basketful of chips would do her the world of good.

'Would you like your drink first?' the man from the bar asked.

'Yes, please.'

'Ice and lemon?' he persisted.

'Ice and orange,' she replied.

When the drink arrived, the Campari had been drowned in soda and was served in a tumbler.

As he approached us, I noticed Mr Tomlinson's hand was trembling. 'You've been up to the Manor,' he said. It was more of a statement than a question.

I made an unsuccessful attempt to deflect it. 'Very sad business about Mr Swinton,' I said.

'How much do you know about what really went on over there?' he asked.

'To be frank, I hadn't heard of Mrs Langhorn until a few days ago,' I replied truthfully.

'Funny lady,' he growled.

'In what way?'

'Used to be a lot of fun when she was young. At least, that's what folks say.'

'You knew her well?'

'I didn't know her at all. No one did, even though she moved into the village soon after the war. I was only a lad at the time, of course.'

'A very private person, was she?'

'Very absent person, I would say.' He laughed at

his own repartee. 'Mind, it wasn't always like that, at least that's what they say. When they first came here, I'm told the Langhorns were out and about quite a bit. They even bought an ambulance and fire-fighting apparatus for the village. And then Mrs Langhorn went around raising money for the war widows. They say she gave most of the lolly to start the old folks' home at the top of the hill. In a funny sort of way the major, her husband, became quite popular. Bit of a wimp, perhaps, but apparently harmless. She was the one with the trousers.'

'Did they come into the pub?' I asked.

'Good God, no. That would have been asking too much. They were never part of the village like that. The most we would ever really see of them was sweeping down the main street in their posh cars, Rolls Royces and the like. Each of them had his own personal chauffeur to take him to the factory in Witney. They were into some sort of chemicals manufacturing: very successful it must have been, though they say they dealt with the workers as if they were their subjects. I'm not joking. They wanted to be treated like King and Queen. I mean it. The managers had to take off their shoes before entering Mrs Langhorn's office and to back out of her presence. At the company dance I'm told there was a ringed-off throne where the staff could pay homage to the Major and Mrs Langhorn, who sat there receiving people all evening. They employed hundreds in the late forties and fifties. No overtime was paid when people stayed late. After seven o'clock you got two slices of bread, a banana and a cup of tea. And then one day it all changed.'

'How did that happen?'

'The major's death. He died suddenly in the summer of 1965. I remember that day as if it was yesterday. It was stinking hot. The cricket team had just assembled at the pavilion for an afternoon match against Moreton-in-Marsh Second Eleven. It must have been about two o'clock. Suddenly an ambulance came screaming up the hill and into the Manor drive. It arrived as suddenly as that one did this morning, only the siren was a bell in those days. I personally never saw either the major or Mrs Langhorn again.'

'She became a total recluse?'

'If that's what they call people who disappear. They say she went on living at the Manor, but I have no proof of it. They say she was the force behind the scene before he died; they say she was a great beauty before the war and a friend of Fred Astaire, a great mover on the dance floor. They say this and that and all sorts of things. But I have no proof. She could have been dead years ago, for all I know.'

'But there is one man who did know?'

For a moment he looked puzzled. 'Who's that?'

'Jack Swinton.'

'Oh, yes, you're right there. But he's dead as well now, poor bugger. The police have been down the road all morning. Hanged himself by the pavilion.'

'I know,' I said.

He looked at me suspiciously.

'How do you know about Jack?' he asked. 'Are you from the government or something?'

'Yes,' I answered, meeting his gaze directly.

'What were they up to up there? On the tax fiddle, were they? I can't say I'm surprised. I was only saying to the missus a few weeks ago that they were probably on the take. Was Jack part of it, poor bugger?'

It was the opportunity I had been waiting for. 'Tell me about Jack,' I said. 'He seems to have been a bit of a loner.'

'How do you know?' he asked sharply.

'I picked it up coming up the hill. There were a number of villagers hanging around the cricket pitch. The general view was that he kept to himself pretty much.'

Mr Tomlinson scratched the side of his mouth.

'Funny bloke,' he said. 'Sometimes I thought I really knew him. He would stay here late some nights, and I mean very late.' And then, presumably remembering I was from the government, he added, 'What I'm saying is that he stayed on more as a private guest than as a customer, no question of breaking the licensing laws, you understand. We're very particular about that in this establishment. You have to be these days. You really can't be too careful. Mind you, I don't know what they're bothered about. With all these drink-drive laws, most people are on bottled water anyway. What a price the manufacturers charge for that, by the way. Bloody criminal. Now I've lost my train of thought. Where was I?'

'Jack Swinton. He used to stay late some nights.'

'Oh, yes. You think you get to know people when they're a bit in their cups. I'm not sure how true this was of Jack. Somehow with him I always felt I was about to be in for a big surprise.'

'And were you?'

He considered the matter. 'I'm not sure. Some things about him were pretty straightforward, at least I think they were, like that he came to live in the village soon after the major's death. Before he moved into the Manor as some sort of general dogsbody, I am pretty certain he worked at the Langhorn's chemical factory.'

'What do you think his job was there?'

'That's the bit I'm not so clear about. The view in the village is that he must have been some sort of a cleaner there. As I say, I'm not so sure. I think he might have been more important. He never admitted it direct, mind. It was just that occasionally he let drop little remarks that made me think that there was more education in him than met the eye.'

'What do you think he was?' I asked.

'It sounds crazy and you'll probably laugh, but I think he had some science in him. Either that, or he was just naturally good at picking up scientific information. Some people are, aren't they? For instance, he could rattle off the letters of fertilizer compounds. He used to do it sometimes just for a lark when one of those fertilizer reps had been in the pub.'

I felt for the moment this was about as far as we were going to get on the subject of Jack Swinton.

'What about the rest of the staff at the Manor?' I asked.

'No idea,' he said. 'They all came and went very quickly and they all seemed to be from out of the village. I seem to remember Jack saying that in recent years there was no one other than himself who lived in, but I really don't know. One or two local folk used to go up there until a few years ago. A chap called Tom Mogg even claims to have had a row with her. I can't recall now exactly what it was about. Tom farms on land alongside the Manor grounds. If I remember rightly, he was accused by some smarty-pants lawyers of hers from London of stealing some of her timber. In the end I think it was discovered that the trees had been cut down on the orders of her own agent. Then there's Dave Lucas, of course. He has some good yarns to tell about the Langhorns. I don't know how many of them are true, but they make good listening. Dave has a camera shop in Moreton-in-Marsh. They used to employ him to take photos of their business in Witney but never, I might say, was he asked to take pictures of the Langhorns themselves. Dave says they were paranoid, if that's the right word, about having their photos taken.' Mr Tomlinson's voice began to trail away. 'Here, I'm prattling on a bit,' he said with newfound reticence.

'Not at all. It's very interesting,' I encouraged.

'It must be your good looks,' he said, with seemingly swiftly restored confidence. 'We don't often get them in here quite as pretty as you. Tends more to be the ruffians off the farms or the pensioners: plenty of old-age pensioners in the village these days. Most of them are newcomers as well. You must be something to do with the winding up of the estate: probate they call it, I believe. They say she didn't leave any heirs. If you've got any say in it, get us somebody nice in the Manor, will you? The village deserves a break on this one. Somebody who likes beer would be perfect. Here, I'd better go and fetch your food, otherwise the chips will be stone cold.'

When he was gone, Pat said, 'I wonder how much of all that is known to the chief?'

'The question is, how much of it is relevant?' I said.

'Relevant to what?' she asked.

'Another good question,' I conceded.

A few minutes later Mr Tomlinson returned with a heavily scratched black plastic tray. On it the sandwiches, the chips and the scampi were piled in no obvious order. He had also thought to include a cracked bottle of vinegar and two of the smallest paper napkins I have seen.

'My missus says you're probably from the police,' he announced. 'I told her, "Impossible, you want to look at them," but the missus says the police come in all shapes and sizes these days. She watches too many American TV shows, if you ask me.'

'Your wife is almost correct,' I said. 'I am a kind of policewoman,' I admitted.

He put down the tray with a clatter and looked directly at me.

'What exactly does that mean?' This rather shocked reaction no doubt meant he was guilty of some misdemeanour; he was probably behind with his tax payments.

'It means that I'm here officially,' I said, I suspect not very reassuringly. If anything, his nervousness grew. The tremor in his hand became a definite shake.

'Is something the matter?' I asked with genuine concern.

He didn't seem to hear this.

'Have you got some sort of proof that you're official?' he asked.

'Will this do?' I flashed my ID card at him.

'This makes a difference,' he said. 'If you're official, there *is* something else that you should know.'

He paused. Pat scraped her chair on the stone floor as she pulled it closer to him.

'It sounds crazy.' He hesitated again. I am an experienced interrogator and I sensed that this was not the moment to prompt him. If I pressed him too hard, he would no doubt blurt out the first thing that came into his head and I would never know what was actually on his mind. Suddenly he crouched down beside me. His voice fell to a whisper.

'Your friend will have no doubt told you that Jack Swinton was in here two nights ago.' He addressed me directly. 'As I say, after a few pints he starts to talk a bit, just to me privately, that is. He doesn't raise his voice or anything like that. He was on about this coloured girl who came to see Mrs Langhorn just before she died.'

'I thought she had olive skin,' I said.

'Olive, brown, what difference does it make? I think Jack said she probably came from one of those Mediterranean countries: Israel, Greece, or even one of the Arab places. One thing he was certain about was that she had something to do with the missus's death.'

'How on earth could he have been sure of that?'

'Apparently she was alone with Mrs Langhorn in her bedroom for over two hours. After the girl had gone, the lady started to act very strangely.'

'She began to retreat even further into herself?'

'No, on the contrary, she came to life, just like she must have been before her husband died. Apparently she couldn't sit still at all. Up and down she was—to phone her bankers in Switzerland, her lawyers, old business associates, anyone who would talk to her. It was as if she knew that time was running out for her, tidying up all her affairs, you might say.'

'That doesn't add up to the fact that she was murdered,' I insisted.

'She had funny friends,' he said.

'Maybe.'

Tomlinson edged closer to me. His breath smelt

of whisky. He paused for a moment, then he said, 'I may as well tell you the whole thing, lady, seeing you're so sceptical. That girl, the coloured one, offered Jack good money to kill Mrs Langhorn.'

'Did he accept?' I asked immediately.

Tomlinson seemed rather shaken by the directness of this question. For a moment he stared straight back at me through eyes which were disturbed.

Then he said, 'Did he what?' There was a sinister, aggressive tone to his voice now.

'Did Jack Swinton kill Mrs Langhorn?'

The publican stood up hurriedly and raised his voice. 'You must be out of your mind. Jack Swinton was a good man. He worshipped the ground Mrs Langhorn walked over. He was hopelessly in love with her, you might say.'

'Why haven't you told all this to the police?' I asked.

His anger changed abruptly to sulkiness. 'Because they never asked me.'

Afterwards I asked myself whether I thought this excuse was entirely credible.

4

'I wonder why Jack Swinton didn't mention his olive-skinned lady to the coroner,' I said to Pat when Tomlinson had left us. 'She certainly doesn't feature in the official report.'

'Perhaps because she was successful,' Pat replied.

'In persuading Swinton to kill Mrs Langhorn?'

'It would fit with the suicide note. What did you say the exact words were? "I am responsible for Mrs Langhorn's death"?'

'Assuming that the cause of Swinton's death was suicide and that he wrote the note himself,' I commented.

'You have doubts about it?'

'His departure from the scene was, to say the least, convenient for Miss Olive Skin if she existed in the form in which she has been presented to us.'

We sat for a moment in silence. Then I said, 'When you've finished those chips, I want to have another go at the Manor. I was interested by what

Tomlinson had to say about the reluctance of the Langhorns to have themselves photographed. It ties in with the complete absence of family snaps around the house. There wasn't even a picture of a pet or of a servant or a friend.'

'Presumably someone removed them,' Pat suggested.

'After Mrs Langhorn died?'

'Could be, or even before.'

'There's only one person who seems to have had a free run of the house before and after her death.'

'Did you search Swinton's room?'

'Not unless he used one of the main bedrooms,' I admitted, 'and I can't say I found male paraphernalia in any of them. I didn't really have time to go through the servants' quarters. It's one of the main reasons I want to go back.'

'I'll come with you,' Pat volunteered. 'Who knows, we might even find more dead bodies.' Her chuckle was rather bloodthirsty and distinctly unladylike.

Back in the Manor we headed straight for the first floor. We began to work our way down a narrow corridor towards the rear of the house, opening every door as we went. The rooms were tiny compared to those in the front of the house. They were also completely empty.

By the time we reached the end of the passage, the light had become very poor.

'Is there a switch anywhere?' Pat asked from in front of me.

'I tried one earlier on,' I said. 'It didn't work. Presumably the bulbs have gone. It all looks pretty unused down here.'

'There's a small staircase on the right. Let's give that a go, shall we?'

I followed her up the narrow winding flight of wooden stairs. These led directly into a small room with a low ceiling and steeply sloping walls, into one of which was cut a narrow lattice window. I took a quick look around. On the far side, under the window, there was an iron bed carefully made up, with a pale-blue sheet turned neatly over the blanket. Next to the bed there was a locker, and beside that was placed a rough yellow wooden chair looking as though it had come straight out of a Van Gogh painting. At the other end of the room there stood a three-drawer pine chest. That was it, except for a small rectangular rush mat under the bed. No curtains, no fitted carpet, no pictures.

'If this was Swinton's room, it's unnaturally clean and tidy, don't you think?' Pat said.

'They say that people who are about to commit suicide like to leave everything shipshape behind them,' I suggested.

'But not like this, surely,' my companion persisted. 'Someone must have cleaned up after him.'

'We aren't even certain that this was Swinton's room,' I cautioned, 'though I agree we've effectively run out of alternatives. Let's take a look around. I'll start with the chest of drawers.'

This was empty except for the top right-hand drawer. Here, rather strangely, I came across four old restaurant bills and an unwashed test tube which rolled noisily to the front as I pulled the drawer out.

'If this was Swinton's room, I wonder where he kept his clothes,' I said.

At that moment Pat gave a long shrill whistle, not totally out of character, but rather untypical of some-one of her age and seniority.

'What's that for?' I asked.

'Come over here, my dear Jane, and take a look for yourself.'

I crossed the room to where she was sitting on the only chair. Taking up a position behind her, I leaned over her shoulder. In her hands lay an old photo album, its cover torn so badly that pieces of leather were hanging from it in shreds. As she thumbed through the pages, I counted twelve black-and-white photographs.

It was immediately clear that there was nothing ordinary about this collection of snaps. The first six in the book had been so badly defaced with a sharp instrument that they were completely unrecognizable. The next four had been treated more carefully. That is to say, the vandal had taken more trouble with them. Instead of slashing wildly at the pictures, as had clearly been the case with the first six, he had clinically cut out the faces of the second group. No mad frenzy this time, merely a calculated circumcision so that head-less bodies stood beside exotic vegetation and leaned against buildings with paneless windows and corru-gated-iron roofs.

Pat turned to the penultimate page. This time the picture was in perfect condition.

'I wonder why he left this one alone?' she said.

'What about the last page?' I asked.

She turned over the final leaf of the book.

'This one's untouched as well.'

'We'll extract the two good ones and have a closer look at them,' I said. 'The lab can analyse the others, though I can't believe they'll be able to make much sense of them.'

Pat carefully detached the unspoilt pictures from the album and handed them over to me. I held one in each hand and faced them towards the window.

In one of them a group of seven men and women sat around a circular table. In the left-hand corner of the photograph were printed the words: 'Taken on board RMS *Queen Mary*.' Three of the men were dressed in dinner jackets; one was in naval uniform. I decided for the moment to concentrate my attention on the two younger members of the group. On the far right of the picture, two places away from the naval officer, presumably the ship's captain, and nearest to the camera, sat a woman in her late thirties. She was strikingly good-looking, though her beauty was the type more likely, I would have thought, to overawe a man rather than to seduce him. Her stretched smile was made with heavily painted lips direct at the camera. The distinct contours of her figure were presented sideways to the photographer. Just below the edge of the table-cloth her long legs were crossed at the ankles. The whole impression was of someone who knew exactly how to work to the camera. Rather incongruously, but adding to the sense one had that her pose was contrived, she held a straw hat in her right hand.

'Funny thing to have at the dinner-table,' Pat said. 'The hat, I mean. I wonder what she did with it when she began to eat.'

'Returned it to the photographer's prop box, I should imagine,' I replied.

'Presumably it is Mrs Langhorn.'

'She certainly fits my idea of what she would have looked when she was younger,' I said.

'Except that she was meant to be camera-shy,' Pat commented. 'That women is acting like a professional model. Look at what she is putting into it: concentrating her entire mind and body on having her picture taken.'

'The impression I have is that she was a bit of a glamour puss until her husband died,' I said. 'Then it all changed radically. I imagine the man with the jolly, rather stupid-looking face talking to the elderly woman across the table is Mr Langhorn. He seems totally unaware that he's being photographed.'

'I can't help feeling that Mr Langhorn's looks are deceptive,' Pat said. 'He must have been a cleverer chappie than he is being cracked up to have been to have run such a successful business, Mrs Langhorn or no Mrs Langhorn.'

I placed the picture on top of the bedside locker.

'What do you make of the other one?' I asked, raising the second of the unspoilt photos to the light.

This time the man and the woman stood by themselves, with their arms linked around each other. Behind them a jetty pointed out to sea. In the top left-hand corner of the photo, palm leaves were suspended above the woman's head. Several years had evidently elapsed between this event and the dinner on the *Queen Mary*. Mrs Langhorn, assuming that was who she was, had put on weight in the intervening period. In the more recent picture, she wore a flimsy dress whose top half was barely able to contain her very rounded bosom. Rather curiously, she was still holding what looked like the same straw hat in her right hand.

'Strange,' Pat muttered.

'About the hat?'

Pat appeared not to hear me. She was staring intently at the beach scene.

'Does anything strike you as peculiar about that picture?' she asked. I studied it more closely and saw immediately what was interesting her.

'The fact that they look so alike?' I suggested.

'It's very odd, don't you think,' Pat pressed. 'In many ways their features are identical. The likeness is not so apparent in the dining-saloon scene. It only really strikes you after Mrs Langhorn has put on weight and her face has rounded out. Look at their mouths and, even more, their noses, both straight and pointed, and the slope of their foreheads, almost identical. And what about the shape of their eyes? Quite extraordinary.'

'It's odd,' I agreed, 'but it could be a little deceptive. Mr Langhorn's face is half hidden by the shadow of his bush hat.'

Pat was not to be put off. 'Well worth noting, though,' she insisted.

'I'll certainly point it out to the chief when I see him,' I said.

'When will that be?' The tone of her voice had suddenly become sharper.

'Tomorrow, I hope.'

'You won't forget to mention my problem to him, will you?'

I smiled. 'I'll certainly do my best, you know that. But it won't, as they say, exactly be for the first time of asking, will it. Every time I bring it up I get a variant on the same response.'

'That he's not currently planning to re-employ former agents over the age of seventy.'

'However good they are at firing off machine guns and kicking men where it hurts them most,' I added.

'What a waste,' she sighed. 'What a terrible waste.'

I did not admit it to her, but deep down I rather agreed. I could think of few agents at present on the office payroll who were mentally as agile as Pat Huntington. What was more, she was in better physical shape than one or two that I could think of, even though on average they were some fifty years younger than she was. For that matter, most of the other agents were now some fifteen or so years younger than me. This hardly meant that they were more effective. I rather sensed that, if anything, I was now at the peak of my powers.

5

'May I take a look myself at the coroner's report?' the chief asked.

We leaned towards each other and I handed him the two closely typed sheets of foolscap paper. He held them in his left hand, lay back on the sofa and stretched out his long legs in front of him. Although his angular, unlined face showed no emotion, I sensed that he was taking a deeper interest in the paper than I would have expected. No reaction from the chief ever came as a total surprise; his unpredictability was part of his effectiveness, not to say his attractiveness. Nevertheless, I could not help thinking that it was rather strange that the death of an eccentric old woman should merit so much of the personal attention of the head of Britain's counter-intelligence services.

As I watched him languidly absorbing the words of the report, I considered—not, I may say, for the first time—how little I really knew about him. Having served under him directly for some eight years, I was, of course, as aware as anyone of his public persona. This was complex enough: on the surface, the aristocratic politeness; not far below, the professionalism, the ruthlessness and formidable intelligence. (He had apparently once considered becoming a Don in Classics at Oxford.) I had firsthand knowledge of his extraordinary ability to adopt different disguises (not only completely altering his facial appearance, but totally transforming his voice to match the particular character). Despite all this, I knew that my appreciation of him was completely superficial. I had not a clue, for instance, about his private life. As I have written elsewhere, I didn't even know whether he was married; nor, as far as I could tell, did anyone else around the office. Presumably his formidable assistant and sentinel over many years, Miss Fry, OBE, knew where he lived. If she did, and even that was not clear, she certainly did not share this information with her fellow employees. As far as I was concerned, I lived each day with the chief as if we were performing in a play together. He was the star. When the curtain came down, he left the stage for another world, of which I was no part.

Actually, the theatrical analogy is an imperfect one. It implies a certain rhythm in our performance. Quite definitely this was not the case. The chief was a man of extraordinarily irregular habits. Sometimes he would spend several days and nights on the trot inside the office building. Then, without warning, he would depart, often for some military airport from where he would go to God knows where, usually in recent years, I would guess, to Northern Ireland.

Suddenly, he seemed to become aware of the closeness with which I was studying him. Raising his grey-blue eyes, he placed the coroner's report on the sofa beside him. He joined his hands and stretched his arms in an arch above his head. For a moment I thought he was going to yawn. That would have been a first for me, to have witnessed him yawn. Instead, he began to address me in his slightly slurred upper-class voice. This barely required him to open his mouth. (Had he chosen to do so, he could have spoken in perfect French or Arabic, not to mention ancient Greek or Latin, in each of which he was supposed to have gained a first-class degree at Oxford.)

'Although the immediate cause of her death was apparently pneumonia,' he said, 'the evidence is quite clear that around the time of her death she had a heavy fall. The body was quite badly bruised. There was a particularly nasty gash on the side of her head. It is certainly possible that some sort of violence was involved.'

'I still don't quite follow why it should matter to us if there was, sir.' No doubt he saw this for what it was: a crude attempt by me to prompt him into giving me a full briefing on the background to the case.

He closed his eyes for a moment. His body sagged into the back of the sofa. I knew from experience that this posture was deceptive. At an instance it could be transformed from that of a relaxed, rather effete-looking intellectual into the rigid, erect form of a professional soldier, which is what he had once been.

He opened his eyes and muttered, 'It's all very difficult.' As if to emphasize the point, he got up and crossed the room to his large Victorian desk. He picked up two documents and brought them over to where I was sitting.

'Take a look at these.' He handed me a piece of printed paper and a battered British passport. 'They were the only records placed for safekeeping by Mrs Langhorn with her lawyers. Because she has apparently left no heirs, the Treasury Solicitor's office have managed to obtain them for us. As you will see, one of them is a relatively recent vaccination certificate, which gives her date of birth as January 22, 1909. However, it's the passport I found the more interesting. As a former policewoman, see what you make of it, Jane.'

It was rare for the chief to refer to my previous job in this way. Nor was it especially apt on this occasion. I had not been a particularly useful member of the Metropolitan Police force. I had joined its ranks too soon after the breakup of my marriage. Indeed, getting a job at all had frankly been a bit of an indulgence on my part. As the divorced wife of Lord John Hildreth, one of the richest men in the world, I certainly did not need the money. What is more, despite the efforts of both John and myself to keep all the arrangements quiet and amicable, the divorce had been widely publicized. So there had been no hope of hiding from my new police colleagues that I owned a cottage in the Cotswolds, a house in Montpelier Square, and an apartment on the Upper East Side, between Park and Madison, in New York. Nor had there been any point in pretending that my life-style had much in common with that of my fellow coppers, most of whom either lived with their mums and dads down the Pentonville Road or shared council flats in Brixton. If I had been enthusiastic about the job, things might have been different. They might have come to respect me, despite my wealth and my title. But I was not and they did not. One or two of the men would, I suspect, have 'fancied a bit on the side with the classy blonde with the sexy little figure' (if so, they were disappointed); most must have just found my presence a 'pain in the arse.' For me it had just been a piece of escapism which led nowhere. I had wanted to show my parents and my former husband that I could stand on my own feet. The truth was that I had not been willing to make the necessary commitment and the experiment was a pretty well unmitigated flop.

Fortunately this was not true of my next job. I was introduced to the counter-intelligence service by the father of a girl I had been at boarding-school with. I began in counter-subversion and then moved to counter-terrorism. More recently I had been switched to counter-espionage. Over a period of ten years I had become one of the most experienced and, I have to admit it, competent agents in the business. That, I suppose, was why I had been drawn closer and closer into central operations, eventually reporting direct to the director-general himself. It also no doubt partly explained why I had not remarried. I freely confess to having had several quite exotic affairs; not that I consider myself to be promiscuous. Most of the romances could, I suppose, have ended in marriage if I had wanted them to. It was not, however, just a question of putting my job first. The fact was that since my abortive relationship with John Hildreth, I had not fallen in love again.

I took a close look at the passport my boss had handed to me. It did not take great powers of detection to see why it had caught his interest. The label on the cover, under the words 'British Passport,' was marked 'Mrs Veronica Langhorn.' Her date and place of birth had been scratched out from the first page and I was not entirely surprised to find that the photograph had been torn out. What was much more interesting was that no one had thought to remove the reference to her maiden name. Apparently this had been 'Harringay.' I lingered over the name for a moment and then turned to the other pages. These were filled with visa and entry stamps from Australia, the United States and, in one case, from the 'Kingdom of Iraq.'

I was conscious of the chief's physical closeness as he leaned over the back of my chair. I turned to look up at him.

'It must have been forged,' he said.

'The passport?'

'Yes. I've checked the records. It was never is-
sued; not, that is, with the name "Langhorn." '

'Why on earth would she have passed a defaced,
and therefore useless, passport to her solicitors for
safekeeping? If she wanted the details to be kept secret,
would it not have been simpler just to destroy the
passport?'

'To that I have as yet no proper answer. I suspect
she wanted to leave a trail behind after her death. It
may have been her way of ensuring that her true identity was never completely lost.'

'At least the missing photo fits the pattern,' I said.

He raised his right eyebrow. 'Meaning?'

'I think you should see these, Chief. I found them
at Studwell.'

I handed him a thin brown envelope.

'Photos?'

I nodded.

He took the envelope into the centre of the room.
Kneeling on the floor, he shook out its contents onto
a glass coffee table. Like a little boy playing with his
toys on the carpet, he was totally absorbed in what he
was doing.

Suddenly he exclaimed, 'That's her!'

Holding up the picture of the group on the *Queen
Mary*, he pointed to the glamorous lady on the far
right of the captain's table.

'That's her,' he repeated. 'That's Mrs Langhorn.'

There was no missing the new thrill in his voice. For a moment the mask had dropped. His discovery had genuinely affected him; for once, the master of disguise was not able, or not willing, to hide his real emotion. I do not deny it, the change in him was of more than passing interest to me. It began to occur to me that he might after all be capable of enjoying a full range of human feelings. There was no question of it, this new mood excited—even, I admit, aroused—me. The fact that I chose not to show it had, on thinking about it, all to do with not making any move which might force him back into his shell. When I spoke, it was in as clinical a tone as I could manage.

'I'm afraid most of the pictures are not going to be much good to us. I've already shown them to the lab. They will do what they can, of course, but clearly they can't restore the bits that have been cut out. I'm not very confident that they will come up with very much.'

I am not sure that the chief heard much of this. Certainly he seemed quite distracted when he muttered, 'I wonder.'

Then, carefully and with great precision, he selected from the table only those photographs from which the faces had been cut out. Uncoiling his long thin body, he rose from the floor and moved over to the window. There, for what must have been a full five minutes, his figure remained motionless, silhouetted against the fast fading London light. His concentration appeared to be complete. The room fell into total silence. It was as if he had forgotten that I was still there.

At last, with a slight click of his feet, he turned round to face me and began to move swiftly back across the room.

'These pictures really are extraordinary,' he said. His voice was firm and clear. 'I'm not too bothered about the one of Mr and Mrs Langhorn standing by themselves on a beach. I imagine that was taken on one of their trips to the Caribbean. I seem to recollect seeing somewhere that they owned property on one of the islands. The interesting photos are without doubt those from which the heads have been removed.'

'You've found a pattern to them?' I asked.

'That's hardly the point,' he answered enigmatically, 'though the youthfulness of some of the bodies is interesting. That one of a small boy could turn out to be particularly relevant. And one of the others has an arm around the one next. I think that could be significant too.'

'So there is something to be deduced from a collection of headless young bodies lounging around a scattering of tin huts?'

'Yes, if you know the place where the photographs were taken,' he said almost slyly.

'But that's hardly possible, Chief. There must be literally millions of comparable sites around the world.'

'Perhaps comparable,' he said, 'but not identical.

These photos were taken in a little town in Western Australia. It's called Broome.'

'How can you possibly be certain about that?'

'There are several clearly recognizable landmarks. Besides, that is where Mrs Langhorn came from.'

He perched himself down on the arm of the chair in which I was sitting and held up the photos in front of me.

'See that building with the tin roof? That's the old cinema. The sandy bits, they're part of Cable Beach. It goes for miles and is often completely deserted, one of the most beautiful spots on earth. It's a great pity that they aren't in colour. The photos, I mean. You don't get the feel from them of the sheer whiteness of the sands and the blood-red of the earth on the banks behind. They can't have been taken at the hottest time of day. Even in black and white, you would sense the shimmering heat. The Australian artist, Sidney Nolan, captures it wonderfully, the heat. Everything in front of you seems to wobble and bend and to go out of focus. That's what makes it easier for a painter to depict than a photographer. I say, the mangrove plantations have grown a bit, but that's the nature of the tree: nothing can stop it if the swamp remains at the right depth.'

'And the headless bodies?' I asked.

'She must have wanted to keep the photos as a memento of the place, perhaps of the particular occasion, while making it impossible for those who were present to be identified.'

The chief seemed to be strangely determined to justify the act of partial vandalism. It was almost as if he were personally involved in some way. Perhaps it was just that he had yet to explain the coincidence of his own knowledge of the place where the photos had been taken.

'When were you last in Broome?' I asked.

'Probably about thirty years ago.'

'It must have impressed you.'

He laughed. There was nothing forced about this. I had never previously thought of associating happiness with the chief, but at that moment that is precisely what he seemed to be, happy.

'It certainly did make a bit of an impression on me, my dear Jane. You see, I was born there.'

Once again a deep silence settled over us. I wondered whether he was as conscious as I was that our relationship seemed to have arrived at some sort of a watershed. For the first time in eight years, for the first time ever, he had allowed me to take a glimpse over the barrier which separated his public from his private existence. It had been brief and inadequate but it had been real. The chief I now knew had been born an Australian, or rather, he had been born in Australia. There was a difference, of course. I wondered whether this put me ahead of Miss Fry. Well, well, well. So where did that leave the upper-class English accent and the languid looks? Presumably they had arrived on the scene at a later date, after he had departed for the Old World; and had that been for good, or was he over here on some sort of temporary assignment? It was all very heady stuff. Is it surprising that I became a little elated, physically, that is, as well as mentally. What, I wondered for the first time, were his other weak spots? Not that there was any question of my entangling myself with these matters too deeply. At least, that is what I told myself. I was embarking on a voyage of fantasy, not of action. For a start, there was the probable complication of a wife. I do not engage, if I can help it, with married men. It has only happened twice in my life, and that was two times too many. Certainly I would scrupulously avoid making any first move. Move towards what? Even to pose the question was to go too far. Or was it? What if he was unmarried? That would make it all rather different, wouldn't it? Perhaps I should ask him outright. I would do no such thing. It might ruin everything before it had begun.

When at last I spoke, I was worried that he might detect the effort in my voice. No doubt I was being over-sensitive.

'Does that mean you might know personally some of the people in the pictures?'

He chose totally to ignore the question, at least I think he did. Later, of course, I understood better the association of ideas.

What he actually said was, 'Mrs Langhorn's forged passport referred to her maiden name as "Harringay." That's a big name where I come from.'

'So she does have a family?'

· 55 ·

This time the shrug was accompanied by a grimace in which he raised his lower lip and dropped the ends of his mouth. This was becoming a little irritating. It seemed more than ever possible that the chief was pursuing a private interest of his own. That would explain why I had been asked to visit Studwell Manor on a Sunday, out of company time.

As if at last reading my thoughts, he said, 'I'm sorry to have spoilt your weekend, especially as there was nothing much to find at Studwell.'

'Only one dead body,' I said, 'though I have accepted all along that that may have nothing to do with our department.'

'Ah, yes. Mr Jack Swinton, who apparently committed suicide after claiming responsibility for Mrs Langhorn's death. He seems to have had what were for him rather catastrophic second thoughts about the whole business, assuming, of course, he was master of his own destiny.'

'What does that mean?' I asked. 'Are you suggesting that he and Mrs Langhorn were both murdered and the note was forged?'

'It's possible, isn't it?'

I had the sense that his mind was not fully focused on the subject; either that or he was being purposely evasive.

Partly in order to try to re-engage his attention, I said, 'And the girl with the olive-coloured skin?'

The chief looked past me towards the door behind which Miss Fry held guard.

'We'll want to look into her, of course,' he said.

'So that's where I should begin?'

'No.'

'There's a better lead-in?'

'Perhaps.'

I waited for him to elaborate. Instead, he turned his back on me and faced towards the window.

'Should I pack my bags for Australia?' I asked.

For a moment he did not answer. There was total silence between us. Then he turned round and looked directly at me. His face was troubled. A line which I had not noticed before creased the lower half of his chin. Suddenly he appeared rather vulnerable. I wanted to immerse myself quickly in whatever it was that was worrying him. It was a wish that I didn't know how to communicate to him.

Then I heard him say, 'I intend to take you off this case. There is so much else to be done.'

He passed a hand over his face. I could see that he was very tired.

6

'The chief was in a very peculiar mood,' I said to Pat.

'That doesn't entirely surprise me.'

I turned sideways and looked closely at her. It had been an unexpected response.

'When this is over we must have a good chat,' I said firmly.

'Okay,' she agreed, 'but this is not exactly the right moment.'

She had a point. We were sitting in the front seats of my Mercedes looking out across a busy car-park towards a crematorium. To our left a mound of dying flowers was just visible above the rim of a yellow skip. It was a depressing sight.

'I thought the idea was to send the flowers to the local hospitals once the funeral was over,' I said, 'not to toss them on the scrap-heap like that.'

'I believe they've stopped doing that at most crematoria,' my companion replied. 'Apparently the association of the flowers with death upsets the older patients.'

I looked at my watch. 'Still twenty minutes to go,' I said.

'The hearse should be here in about ten minutes,' Pat responded.

On the right-hand side of the car-park, in the middle distance, puffs of black smoke rose at regular intervals from chimneys rising from two modern brick-built chapels.

Pat said, 'They seem to be dispatching bodies at the rate of one every fifteen minutes.'

'It's all very precise,' I agreed.

'Rather like those rides at Disney World,' she added.

I saw what she meant. The procedure was certainly very clear. The mourners assembled five minutes before the start, underneath a Grecian-style portal. Twenty minutes later they emerged blinking into the daylight from a discreet door at the side. Each group was a homogeneous whole, with its members dressed uniformly, according to social class: the higher the class of the group, the more abandoned its dress. At the lower end, pretty girls in short black skirts and matching stockings were escorted by thin young men with two-tone black ties. Farther up the scale the dress deteriorated to blazers and raincoats.

At the end of ten minutes, Pat said, 'It must be our turn next. That's presumably Mrs Langhorn's hearse drawing up now.'

We left the car and began to walk up a short gravel road. A light drizzle made me shiver.

There were only two people in attendance as we approached the door of the chapel. One was a vicar and the other a girl in a smart grey suit. The crispness of her clothes and her generally confident manner suggested that she was part of the establishment.

As we came up to them I heard the vicar say, 'If it wasn't for this, I'd be in France today: Le Mans. I like a bit of motor racing.' He spoke with a cockney accent.

The girl didn't seem to feel the need to respond to him directly. After a few moments she said, 'At least we've got the new automatic doors to work properly. You shouldn't have any bother with them this time. I have to admit, though, we're still having trouble synchronizing them with the music tapes.'

At close quarters I saw that she was rather pretty, though she looked too young to be in charge.

Suddenly noticing us, the vicar stubbed out his cigarette and ran a hand through his balding hair.

'Mrs Langhorn's?' he asked.

'That's right,' Pat replied, matching his casualness. 'We seem to be the only ones here.'

'Looks like it,' the vicar cheerfully conceded. 'She can't have had many friends, can she. The arrangements with me were made through the police. She died a week or so ago, I believe. I haven't been given any details about her life. Would one of you two ladies like to provide me with a few thoughts?

Alternatively, perhaps we could skip the eulogy and fill the five minutes allotted for it with prayers.'

'I should stick to prayers,' I said. 'Her life was rather too complicated to compress into a couple of sentences.'

'Foreign, was she?' he asked.

'Why do you ask that?'

'It was the impression I had from the police, that's all. Up to no good, it seems. Still, it's all over now, God rest her soul, whatever it was that she got up to. Are you solicitors?'

'No, we're not solicitors,' I said.

'That's all right then. You just look like solicitors, that's all.'

'When do we start?' I asked, suddenly feeling a strong desire to get the whole thing over as quickly as possible.

He pulled back the sleeve of his cassock and consulted his watch.

'Just over a minute and a half. The service before ours will have ended two minutes ago; as you can probably hear, our music tape has just begun. You might as well take your seats.'

We accepted this advice and went through the sliding doors. I heard the vicar say to the girl in the grey suit, 'At least your music tapes are working.'

The room we entered was modern and bleak. It contained about ten rows of wooden chairs. We chose places half-way up the aisle.

'Plastic flowers on the altar,' Pat whispered.

After a minute, the doors slid open again and a plain light wood coffin was carried forward on the shoulders of two men in black coats, one of which was covered in dandruff. The vicar took up the rear. As the small procession reached the altar, there was a humming sound from behind us and the doors opened once more. A young woman came in and stood for a moment looking towards the coffin. Her face was partly covered by a shawl. She wore a coat which went down to her calves and which covered the rest of her clothes. She stooped a little, so it was hard to gauge her height. I could see that she had a dark complexion. As she took a seat in the back row, her eyes closed. I imagined she must be praying.

'This could be what we came for,' I said. 'We'll talk to her immediately after the service.'

The vicar said, 'Let us pray.' We leaned forwards against the chairs in front of us.

'Forasmuch as it hath pleased Almighty God of his great mercy to take unto himself the soul of our dear sister here departed . . . sure and certain hope of the resurrection to eternal life . . . who shall change our vile body that it may be like unto his glorious body . . .'

I closed my eyes and considered for a moment what, if he wanted it, would be the last boat train the vicar could catch that night. I was not even sure whether the racing at Le Mans was a two-day event.

'I heard a voice from heaven saying unto me, "Write, from henceforth blessed are the dead." '

'Lord have mercy upon us.'

'Christ have mercy upon us.'

We were getting pretty close to the end of our ten-minute slot.

'The grace of our Lord Jesus Christ and the love of God and the fellowship of the Holy Ghost, be with us all evermore.'

I stood up as the coffin began to slide on a conveyor belt towards a small opening to the left of the altar. It may have been my imagination, but I thought I could hear the furnace roaring in the distance. When the coffin was gone, I turned round. The girl had disappeared.

'Quick,' I said to Pat, 'we mustn't lose her.'

As we began to move towards the back of the chapel, the vicar called after us, 'You can't use those doors. Everyone has to go out through the side door. It's the system. Everything would come to a grinding halt if people started to go backwards. Anyway, the doors at the rear are locked electrically while the coffin is leaving.'

There was no alternative but to follow his instructions.

When we came out we were at the back of the building.

'We've got to get round to the other side,' I said.

It must have taken us a full minute to run round the outside of the building. By the time we reached the front, it did not surprise either of us that the woman was gone.

'She'll be half-way back to Arabia by now,' Pat said.

'I wonder why she came at all,' I muttered.

'To make sure that the remains of her victim were well and truly destroyed?'

'That would have been a bit unnecessary,' I said. 'There were other ways she could have verified that without taking the risk of putting in a personal appearance. I suspect she was checking up on who were the other mourners.'

'In that case she must have been a bit disappointed with the turnout,' Pat said.

As we walked back to the car, I said, 'Now I want to talk to you about the chief.'

'Ah, yes,' she muttered a little unhelpfully.

'Let's discuss it over dinner,' I insisted.

'Alexiou's?'

'Suits me,' I said. 'I could certainly manage moussaka and meze.'

As Pat knew, the little Greek restaurant in my home village of Chipping Campden was one of my favourite eating places. It was ideally suited to the conversation I thought I was about to have with her. As it turned out, this talk took a very different course from the one I had expected, and the consequences certainly were totally unforeseeable.

7

Three hours after leaving the crematorium, I sat opposite Pat beside a fire which consisted of two small logs burning on a brick surface about a metre above the ground. Some of my earlier determination to unburden myself of my latest thinking about my boss seemed to have evaporated. Perhaps it was the sedating effect of the heavy Greek wine, but I was finding it hard to introduce the subject at all. This was most unusual. I had never before found any difficulty in raising with Pat an issue that was worrying me. Deep down I knew that I desperately wanted to discuss with her the chief's recent behaviour. For a while we sat in silence.

At last, presumably sensing the block I was having in introducing the subject, Pat suddenly asked, 'So what happened between the two of you yesterday?'

'It's the Langhorn business,' I replied at last, greatly relieved by the prompting. 'For some extraordinary reason it seems to have got to him. It's making him act out of character.'

'Really?' Was there a hint of the whimsical in her question?

'He's not himself at all at the moment,' I persisted. She took a sip of wine. A single flame from the fire reflected itself in her lovely brown eyes.

'In what way out of character?' she asked.

'Some sort of a barrier has come down between us,' I said.

'I thought barriers were a way of life with the chief,' she volunteered. 'Would you have it any other way? Imagine how difficult things would be if he became personally involved with each member of his staff. I'm not talking about emotionally, of course. He has to be very tough with those below him sometimes. He's bound to keep himself remote. It's why he's so good at the job.'

'What's wrong with being emotional sometimes?' I asked, probably raising my voice a little. She looked straight back at me.

'Now *you're* acting out of character, Jane. What *did* happen at yesterday's meeting?'

A dish of moussaka was placed in front of me. I poked my fork into a piece of aubergine. I didn't feel very hungry any more.

'He's taken me off the Langhorn case, that's what happened,' I said. As I remember, my voice had become quieter, more composed.

'How odd.'

'He probably has his reasons,' I added hurriedly.

Pat smiled openly and fingered an olive in a dish by her side.

'I'm sure,' she said.

'We need to help him, Pat.'

'Help him?' Her surprise seemed genuine. 'Why help him? It sounds to me as if he's been behaving most unreasonably. It's we that need the help, not him.'

Now that I had her interest, I was inclined to pursue the matter.

'It's precisely because he's acting unreasonably that he needs help,' I said somewhat illogically. 'He's in some sort of trouble, I'm sure of it. I can *feel* it. You know what, I think it's something to do with Australia. For some reason, the photos of the Langhorns in Australia have unsettled him. He was born in Australia. It's the first piece of hard information I have ever been able to pick up from him about his private life.'

'Australia?' The word seemed to shock Pat. The smile faded from her lips. Her face went quite pale. For a moment I thought I was about to witness the unthinkable, the Honourable Patricia Huntington passing out.

Her voice was slightly breathless when she asked, 'So he mentioned where he was born?' Her speech became slower and more deliberate. 'In that case, my dear Jane, far from the barriers going up, in your case they've been ripped down. It will be very hard for them ever to be resurrected. To my knowledge, he has never mentioned his Australian roots to anyone else over here, and that includes Miss Fry.'

'I'm not following this at all,' I protested. 'He's obviously mentioned it all to you, Pat. What on earth is going on? I'm totally lost.'

Suddenly she looked very tired and for once almost as old as her years.

'I'm going to have to admit one or two things to you, Jane,' she said. 'I'm afraid that some of what I have to say may come as a bit of a shock. All I can claim is that I didn't plan it this way. As he has spoken, I must take it as a signal that I should do so as well. I owe at least that to our friendship, yours and mine, I mean. I just hope that by speaking I am doing the right thing for you both; that is certainly my intention.'

She paused to acknowledge the smile of a near neighbour sitting two tables away. After that, it all began to flow out.

'The truth is,' she said, 'that I've known your boss ever since he was a small boy. When he grew up, it was I who introduced him to the service.' She paused for a moment. I thought she had lost her train of thought. Then she said, 'I'm hesitating because I am trying to sort out what I want to tell you into some sort of logical order.'

'Why not start at the beginning, with the day you first came across the chief?' I suggested. The interrogator in me had for a brief moment reasserted itself.

'No, I'll go one better than that. Let me begin with myself. I think you'll soon see the relevance. As I recollect, I did once tell you I spent a good deal of my time both before and after the war in Australia. My job there was to do my bit to train up their Special Forces. The point is that much of this work took place in the remoter northern parts of Western Australia. You see, it has all the right sort of inhospitable terrain: crocodile swamps, desert, rock, rough coastline, killer snakes, the lot. Wonderful for training in our sort of work.'

As she talked, memories returned to me of the time when Pat had been my instructor. It had always seemed to be raining. Whether we had been living in peatbogs, climbing mountains or running bare-foot across fields of Welsh bracken, we had always been wet.

Suddenly I heard her say, 'But I'm afraid there is one thing I did not tell you. You see, I'm partly Australian myself. That is to say, a large chunk of my family settled there at the end of the last century and managed to grab vast tracts of land for themselves. I spent a good deal of my late teens over there. My cousins taught me almost everything I know about living rough in the bush. For a while the outback was more than my second home: it was where I felt I really belonged. Later on I even persuaded the family to allow me to use some of their land for the Special Forces training. So I was able, as it were, to live over the shop. It all tied up rather well.'

'I think I can guess where some of this is leading,' I said. 'Did you ever come across a place called Broome?'

'Of course. I knew it very well, though from what I hear it's a very different town today from the place I knew. When I was last there it was nothing much more than a collection of tin huts inhabited mainly by Japanese pearl divers, many of whom managed to get themselves killed by sea snakes. Even the Abos gave Broome a wide berth. It was a dry, soulless sort of place, even though it was close to some fabulous beaches and coral reefs every bit, by the way, as magnificent as those on the other side of the continent.'

I could no longer resist asking the question which, not unnaturally perhaps, had been at the forefront of my mind for the last few minutes.

'So you knew the Harringays?'

'Of course. Everyone knew them. They were the richest family in the area after my own.'

'God,' I exclaimed, 'this really is bizarre.'

'I haven't quite finished yet,' Pat said.

'Did you know that Mrs Langhorn's maiden name was Harringay?' I asked.

'No, I did not,' she replied at once.

'And when I tell you that the chief recognized his old home town of Broome in those pictures we found in Studwell, you will understand why my head's in a bit of a twirl. And anyway, Pat, what about the chief's family? Did you know them?'

She paused and looked directly at me. I felt that we were entering dangerous country.

'I knew them very well,' she said quietly.

'And what were they called?'

'I'm afraid I'll have to leave him to tell you his real name. What I will say is that I introduced him to the service when he decided to leave the army.'

'He was in the British army?' I asked as innocently as I could.

'Not initially. He transferred from the Australian forces through an arrangement with the SAS. I'm sure you know that he ended up commanding them.'

I had certainly heard the rumour that he had.

'That was presumably when he lost his Australian accent?' I asked.

'Strangely enough, he never had much of an accent. You see, he went to school over here when his mother died at the end of the war. She died of pneumonia, poor girl. For a while I acted as his guardian.' She smiled to herself. 'I wasn't much good at it, I have to admit. I always seemed to be too busy. I think, by the way, Jane, I have said all I want to say for the time being.'

'Let's give coffee a miss,' I suggested. 'I can see you're tired, and clearly I have some thinking to do.'

I paid the bill and we walked out of the restaurant together. We parted at the end of the road. I watched her cross the street to her cottage, from which for several years now she had guarded the approaches to my house. The long, flowing dress she had put on for the cremation didn't really suit her. I much preferred her in the denim overalls which she usually wore when she was at home. The dress somehow seemed to age her.

When she reached the middle of the road, she appeared suddenly to recollect something she had forgotten. She turned round and began to walk back towards me. The moon was shining on her face. It made her hair look very grey.

When she was close enough to me, she said, 'Why don't we visit Australia together. I would like to go back to my roots before I die.'

It was the first time I had ever heard her accept her own mortality. Normally she talked of old age in the third person; it was something that happened to other people, but never to her.

'You're due for some leave,' I heard her say. 'And I think you would find many of the answers to the questions you are asking yourself down under. We both know I am not just talking of the Langhorn case. If you want to know more about him, Australia would not be a bad place to start. I have a very special cousin who has a cattle station just outside Perth. We could stay with him for a few days. You'll love him. Amongst other things, he's wonderfully indiscreet.'

Without considering the consequences, I said, 'Okay, when shall we go?'

'How about the day after tomorrow?'

The years were now dropping away from her by

the second. It was a very different Pat from the one who had started to cross the road who completed the journey five minutes later. The spring in her step meant that it was my turn to smile.

8

Lord Huntington was a big man who seemed to make it a habit to wear a large straw hat inside his house. Beneath its wide brim his face was clean-shaven and square-cut. Despite the heavy quantities of beer which he seemed to consume, his features and, indeed, his whole body, were well-proportioned. He was big, but not fat. His face was fully fleshed but not heavy-howled. He looked rather younger than his sixty-odd years.

'Youthfulness seems to be a family characteristic,' I had remarked to Pat when I had first met him at Perth Airport.

I watched him now, as he sat on the veranda gently swaying himself in a large rocking chair, his right hand clasped around a tin of Foster's beer. He stared out into the wide abyss of his estate. When he spoke, his voice was deep and measured. It lent authority to what he said.

'I've lived here nearly all my life,' he intoned, 'and my father before me, but I still miss the trees of England. The land around here is all right for horse breeding. You can even make a living from it with cattle. But it's so empty. I sometimes think I'll pack up even now and go and live with Cousin Pat. If it hadn't been for my patients, I might have done it years ago. The farming has never really interested me, though over the years we've been pretty successful at it because we've been able to pick first-class managers. It's medicine which has kept me out here. I've been a bit unusual even in that. I never practised much in Perth. When I think of it, I've had the country districts pretty much to myself over the years. You might say I was one of the first of the flying doctors. It was an expensive business when I started. You had to buy your own plane, of course. It all became much more developed on the other side and in the centre of the country. Around here I was the only one using an aeroplane for many years.'

He broke off as Pat emerged from behind a pair of louvered doors to our left. She was wearing a loose-fitting khaki tunic and matching trousers.

'You look wonderfully relaxed,' he said. 'What about a drink?'

She smiled. 'As long as it isn't that frightful canned beer. England is beginning to drown in it. Every television commercial break seems to have something to say about Australian beer.'

'Probably because it's good,' he suggested.

'I dare say. But mine's a whisky and soda, if you don't mind, Mick dear.'

I still hadn't fully adjusted myself to his Christian name. To me Micks were small people, and certainly not lords. The other thing I found rather surprising about him was that he had never married. Both physically and in terms of his kind and easygoing character, he seemed rather attractive to me.

'I'll get it myself,' he said, rising from the chair. 'Mrs Sims is busy in the kitchen and Jimmy has the day off. Sit yourself between Jane and me, Pat. I was just telling Jane that I might still pick up sticks and come and live over your way. I've kept that land near Cirencester, you know.'

'Are you thinking of retiring?' Pat asked with some disdain.

'When I'm seventy,' he said.

'Far too early,' Pat snorted. 'I'm seventy-six and should still be on full pay and rations if it weren't for our ridiculous civil service rules. Our office used to be insulated from that sort of bureaucratic nonsense. But gone are those days. Now it's all nine to five and back to the mortgaged house in West Byfleet in time for high tea and the six-o'clock news. Spying at night is out these days.'

He smiled and patted her on the shoulder.

'I'll go and fetch that whisky and another Campari for her ladyship.'

'What a man,' Pat said when he was gone. 'Do

you know, he completely sorted out my back problem after lunch. He's particularly good after he's had a few drinks. He says it makes him lighter on his feet when he starts trampling over you.'

When Mick Huntington returned, he said, 'I think we had better go inside now. The mosquitoes will start to bite the hell out of us in a few minutes.' Two hours later we sat around an oval table. The bottle of claret was almost empty. Mick Huntington smoked contentedly on a large cigar. I poured out another cup of coffee and passed the pot to Pat.

'So you knew the Harringays,' I stated.

He puffed a circle of smoke towards the ceiling, where it was ruthlessly destroyed by a large fan.

'I knew them very well. The old man was a patient of mine until they went to live in the north. Even then I used to visit him a bit, especially when he started to fade away. I was there just after he died, as a matter of fact. He must have been a pretty good businessman, old Joe Harringay, at the beginning of the century. He personally built up the largest oil and chemicals business on the west coast.

'And the rest of his family?'

'I never knew his wife. I believe she died when he was a young man, around the time of the First World War.'

'So what happened to the children?'

He paused. His eyelids flickered for a moment. When he spoke again, his voice was much lower. It was almost as if he did not wish to be overheard, although there were only the three of us in that part of the house.

'There were two. Veronica and John.'

'Were you friendly with both of them?'

He shook his head. 'I never met John. Nor did the family ever refer directly to him. I always assumed he was killed in the last war.'

'And Veronica?'

Again he seemed to falter. When he spoke, he seemed to be choosing his words carefully.

'Veronica was about twenty years older than me. I first met her soon after I had qualified from medical school in the mid-fifties. She was still a very beautiful woman and I have to tell you I fell in love with her. For a few weeks we even became lovers. I was very young and she was very dominant and worldly-wise. It's the old story. It was all hopeless, of course, not just because of the difference in our ages, but also because at the time she was married and living in England. She only ever came back to Australia to see her father.'

He fell silent for a moment, then he added, 'As a matter of fact, the whole thing was so painful from my point of view that when she left to return home, I purposely lost touch with her. It was easier that way. I only know of one occasion when she returned, before her father's death in 1970. I made a point of keeping well away on that occasion.'

'And her surname at the time that you knew her was Langhorn?' I asked.

He put down his glass and looked at me with what seemed to be genuine surprise. 'I haven't heard that name for thirty-odd years,' he said.

'So you weren't aware that she was dead?' I pressed.

'Not for certain. Though I assumed she probably was. She would have been getting on a bit by now; we all are.'

'Mrs Langhorn's death is the main reason for my visit to Australia,' I said. As I did so, I thought back to the telephone conversation I had had with the chief just before leaving. His final words had been, 'By all means take a holiday with Pat, but if it has to be Australia, don't try any clever business on the Langhorn case. I meant what I said; it's not yours any more, Jane. I have another team working on it.'

Mick Huntington twisted the stem of his wine-glass.

'She was a beautiful woman,' he repeated. 'In fact, I never met anyone else to match up to her. I suppose she had everything for me: sex, intelligence, even the mother bit. My own mother died when I was very small. I grew up almost without female contact in English boarding-schools and in a range of large country houses owned by other people. Veronica was the first and, I suppose, the only woman I ever knew. Of course, I didn't really know her. It's an absurdity to suggest that I did, but she did leave behind enough material in my mind for me at least to be able to fantasize about her.'

A large flake of ash fell from his cigar onto the polished mahogany table-top. It broke into a variety of smaller shapes which he began to scrutinize as if the little grey particles held some message for him from the future. Far, far away, a dingo howled. The room itself was silent except for the buzzing of two mosquitoes around a candle flickering in the middle of the table.

Suddenly Pat asked, 'Is there anyone else still living who knew her well?'

For a moment Mick Huntington made no response. I wondered whether he had heard her. He maintained his gaze at the spot where the ash had fallen. Then he looked up and stared straight across at Pat. For a moment he contemplated the handsome aristocratic head with its strands of grey hair falling almost seductively across the forehead.

Then he said, 'There's Cousin Laurence.'

'I thought he was in prison,' she said.

He shook his head. 'They let him out. I believe they dropped the charges against him. Apparently he did some sort of deal with the authorities, turned Queen's evidence. I think that means he shopped some big drugs baron he was tied up with. Not an awful lot has come out in the press. I just hear the rumours like everyone else. I tried to get in touch with him when he was first arrested in Sydney, but he didn't respond to any of the letters I wrote to him.'

'So you don't know what he's up to at the moment?' Pat asked.

'I imagine he's back running his building- and construction business. They say it's flourishing. Which of course makes it all the more tragic that he became involved with the drugs people. As I'm sure you know, Pat, it's by no means the first time that young Laurence has been in trouble with the law.'

'And you believe he kept up some sort of contact with Mrs Langhorn?'

'I know he did.'

'They were friends?'

'No. They were business associates.'

'Are you certain?'

'Yes. He once tried to get me involved, but for the reasons I have already given you, I didn't want to have anything more to do with Veronica. It would have been agony for me. I simply wasn't up to it.'

'But Cousin Laurence went ahead?'

'I believe so.'

'You don't know what sort of business they were in?'

He shook his head.

'I wasn't interested. It was not for me.'

'We must meet him,' Pat said.

Huntington looked at her wearily.

'I'm sure you realize that that won't be easy,' he said.

'Nothing ever is in our business,' Pat chuckled.

'The chief told us to keep off Langhorn territory,'

· 81 ·

I reminded her. She responded with a smile. I had not seen her in such good form for many months.

I heard her say, 'I think I'll have one of your nice cigars, Mick dear. Pity not to round off such a good evening in style.'

9

'This is an honour.' The man who rose to greet us from behind a large pseudo-Victorian desk had fading red hair cut in a fringe. He was in his shirt sleeves, and wore no tie.

The pretty Asian girl in a tight black miniskirt, who had shown us in, asked, 'Will you have coffee?'

I shook his hand. It was damp and limp. Somehow it seemed to match a smile made from narrow eyes and thin lips.

'Yes, please,' I said to the girl.

'Sad news about Veronica,' he said. 'Fancy your being a friend of hers, Pat. I must say, dear, you are positively timeless. When did we last meet? It must have been some twenty years ago, when you were doing some hush hush job for the British government. You look younger than you did then. Let's all sit down, shall we.'

He lay back in a large armchair, placing his feet on the desk in front of him. We perched on two uncomfortable dining-room-type chairs on the other side of the desk. He ran his eye unashamedly up and down my body and then turned to Pat.

'So you're both on holiday here. How long do you plan to stay?'

'As long as it remains interesting,' Pat answered. 'We've got open return tickets.'

'I'd like to show you some of the things I'm doing,' he said. 'Remember Broome? I've got some massive projects under way there. The whole place was opened up by a fellow countryman of ours, Lord Alistair McAlpine. He put the old place on the map when he started a fabulous wildlife park there. I'm taking over where he left off. For starters I've almost finished building an airport which will take 747s. I plan that Broome will become the major gateway to the country, especially for the latest generation of non-stop jets from Britain. They'll be able to make the north-west without refuelling, but not south-east. It will switch all the future development of the country from the right-hand bottom corner to the opposite end.'

'I believe Joe Harringay died there,' I said.

For a moment Laurence Huntington looked startled. Then he said, 'Now you mention it, I think he did die in Broome.' He pulled a wooden box across the desk towards him and extracted from it a large cigar. 'Poetic justice in a way. I'm afraid he was the indirect cause of a lot of other people's deaths in and around the town.'

I must have raised an eyebrow.

'Pearl diving. It's a very dangerous game on that coast. Too many poisonous sea snakes. Their bite can kill you in under a minute if it's in your throat. The cemetery up there is full of Japanese pearl divers, many of whom were employed in their time by Joe Harringay.'

'And now his daughter's dead,' I said. 'I believe you kept in touch with each other almost to the end?'

His eyes narrowed. 'Was that a question or an observation?' he asked.

The spots on his chin had begun to shine, as if reflecting some early-warning mechanism inside him. I realized my mistake in having pressed him too hard and made an attempt to put the matter right.

'Pat has mentioned that she thought you had remained friends.' I tried to sound as vague and uninterested as possible.

'Mick was her lover,' he said. 'I just did a little business with her.'

He paused and I let him continue.

'She kept a small interest in some of her father's old concerns and I did my best to keep an eye on things for her over here.'

Suddenly he withdrew his feet from the desk and rose from his chair. He walked over to a large picture window and looked down across a freeway towards the ocean. Then he turned to face us.

'I really would like to show you my place in Broome, Pat. It isn't often that we are visited by relations from England. And you can bring your pretty friend Jane. She will be able to ask questions to her heart's content. Ansett do a regular scheduled service up there. But if you would rather fly with me in my private jet, you would be very welcome. It's a bit cramped and the lavatory is always full of baggage, but it's at your disposal if you want it.'

As we left the tall modern building in which his office was situated, Pat said, 'It's hard to believe he was once a commissioned officer in the Coldstream Guards. You would have thought he would have at least put on a tie to meet us, never mind a jacket.'

'You'll take up his offer?' I asked. 'Including the trip in his aeroplane?'

'If we must. I don't like being critical of a relation, but he gives me the creeps. I hope we won't regret getting tied up with him, even if it is only for a weekend.'

Pat seemed to have forgotten these forebodings as we reported on time two days later to the General Aviation terminal at Perth Airport. We had been invited to arrive at 'around eleven.' Mick Huntington had, however, brought his white Range Rover to a halt outside the main door of the small building at ten-thirty, 'just to be on the safe side.'

'Talking about safety,' Mick said as he opened the passenger door for me, 'be careful of that so-and-so. I wouldn't trust him closer than the length of a disinfected barge-pole. That's why I'm not coming in with you. I really can't bear to be in his presence these days.' He helped Pat out of the back seat of the car and then handed me my small overnight bag.

'Don't worry, my dear Mick,' Pat said. 'We'll look after ourselves.'

There was merriment in her eyes as we walked together the few yards towards the terminal. Once inside, we had our first surprise of the day. Standing by the reception desk were Laurence Huntington and the pretty little Asian girl who had brought our coffee in his office two days earlier.

'I didn't really introduce you to my wife the last time we met,' he said. 'This is Emily. We got married in Hong Kong about six months ago.'

The girl bowed slightly, but did not smile. Laurence looked, if anything, more jaded than at our last meeting. He was wearing a striped sports shirt which was soiled with sweat patches across the chest and around his armpits. His light-fawn trousers were creased. His hair was cut even shorter than I remembered it. The part just above the ears was greying and I began to wonder whether the rest was perhaps a toupee.

'The pilot tells me we're in for a smooth flight,' he said. 'So we may as well get going.'

Without waiting for our response, he began to head for a glass door on the other side of the room. Emily followed obediently behind him. Like his cousin Mick, he was a big man, though whereas his lordship's waist was lean and sleek, the man in front of me had a pot-belly and a large behind. It contrasted not a little with the almost non-existent bottom of his wife.

As we boarded the Hawker Siddeley 125, I had no difficulty in deciding that the best-looking man on the aircraft was going to be the pilot. He was dressed in a light-blue denim shirt, jeans and matching cowboy hat, droopy dark glasses and even droopier moustache. I only hoped his mastery of aviation was as good as his appearance, though I think on balance I would have preferred to see him in a dark-blue uniform with the odd gold ring around his sleeve. Pat eyed him slowly up and down as she entered the plane and I wondered whether that meant that she shared my reservations. As it turned out, these were misplaced. The thousand-mile flight passed by without technical misadventure.

Once we were in the cabin of the aircraft, Laurence Huntington chose one of the two seats facing the flight deck. I sat opposite him. Pat placed herself on the other side of the small gangway in the seat opposite mine. Mrs Huntington sat on her own amongst the baggage at the back of the cabin outside the small loo. This, as we had been duly warned, was virtually inaccessible. The seat opposite Pat was for some reason left empty. Just as we were, I thought, about to take off, another man climbed aboard and went straightforward to the flight deck, shutting the door firmly behind him. I caught a glimpse of the skin of the back of his neck. This was either very heavily tanned or it was black.

Laurence Huntington loosened the belt of his trousers and stretched out his legs so that I had to pull mine close into my seat. I was glad I was not wearing a tight skirt. The loose-fitting white cotton dress I had chosen for the journey was in the circumstances definitely more appropriate.

Without warning, the little aeroplane began to taxi towards the runway.

'Once we're airborne, Emily will pour us out some champagne,' Huntington shouted above the rising roar of the engines. He then seemed to fall into a deep sleep; stupor might have been a better word.

An hour later he awoke and immediately inquired, 'Did you ever meet Veronica's husband?'

I shook my head.

'Neither did I. I couldn't tell you anything about him except that he died about twenty years ago and was a pretty good businessman. All my dealings have always been with her. I don't even know where he came from. I think you'll find that dear Cousin Mick is as clueless about the matter as I am.' (I checked this up for myself at a later date and discovered that on this point at least Laurence Huntington was speaking the truth.)

'She was bizarrely secretive about him,' he went on. 'I once asked her to send me a photograph of him. I needed it for some sort of promotional purposes. I got no response at all, although she was normally ultra-efficient over business matters. She was very careful to make sure that I never saw him on the very occasional visits I made to the UK. When Veronica and I met, it was always in London and on our own. She never asked me down to their place in the Cotswolds, though I tried on two occasions to elicit an inviation from her. The life she ran there was completely cut off from her Australian friends and relations.'

I wondered briefly why he was supplying me with all this unsolicited information, most of which I assumed was untrue.

'Talking of her relations,' I asked, 'what about her brother?'

'What about him? Let's have that champagne now, Emily.'

'I understood he disappeared in the war.'

'So did I,' he said unhelpfully and lapsed into a silence which lasted for most of the rest of the journey.

About an hour later the aeroplane suddenly banked sharply to the right, revealing a coastline of white sand, behind which the olive green of the mangrove swamps gave way to the red earth of the northern Australian desert. As I looked out of the small porthole beside me, I became conscious out of the corner of my eye that he was watching me.

Suddenly he said, 'There was a time when she would talk about nothing else but her brother. She had an obsession about an affair he had once, shortly before the war, with the wife of a family friend who had a ranch to the south of Perth. The woman was apparently very beautiful, very sophisticated, very bored and very randy, so young John took his chances. For some reason it deeply upset his sister. She never stopped talking about it for many years. I imagined she was angry with her brother for having screwed around with a married lady. As it was, the marriage broke up soon after John went off to war.'

Pat leaned across the aisle and asked, 'What was the woman's surname?'

He looked straight back at her. 'Beverley,' he said. 'They've both been dead for a long time now.'

Pat turned away from him and stared out of the window beside her. Huntington closed his eyes and seemed once more to go back to sleep. The aircraft dipped forward and began to lose altitude. When she turned back towards me, I was astonished to see the redness in Pat's eyes. A tear dribbled down her cheek. She reached into the folds of her denim skirt and pulled out a handkerchief and blew her nose. I had never seen her like this before and we had known each other now for over ten years. She must have seen the surprise in my face because she pulled out a small pad from the top pocket of her tunic and began to write on it in pencil. After a few moments she passed the pad over to me. On it were written the words, 'Beverley is the chief's surname. That woman was his mother.'

10

A young couple sat on a rock behind me. They were dressed in almost identical T-shirts and denim shorts. The young man had red hair and a beard. The girl had long brown hair and a snub nose. I heard the young man say, "The good news is that there aren't many sea snakes around this year. The bad news is that they've all been eaten by the crocs." He spoke in an upper-class English accent. Their laughter was soft and innocent.

In front of me across the surf the sun was setting fast. The green of the ocean was turning to blue and dappled gold. The red rocks on my left were changing to a deep purple. I walked towards the water in my bare feet and thought of the chief. Finally I had learned his name: Beverley. It had a feminine ring about it, not really suited to him, at least to what I knew of him. I wondered for a moment whether I might later discover that it was no longer his name, that he had changed it by deed poll: the ultimate disguise. For the present, I could assume his name was Beverley. It was all I had to go on. The next move was to find out his Christian name. Pat would know it, of course, but Pat was out of bounds so far as this exercise was concerned. There was no question of embarrassing her by asking her. This was between me and him. And who was he? A man whose motive for wanting to take me off the Langhorn case was now somewhat suspect. I had discovered that his mother had had an affair before the war with Mrs Langhorn's brother. Perhaps it was not so surprising that he had sent me to Studwell Manor outside company time. The question now was how best to use the information. I wanted to catch him, not to harm him, but I wanted to catch a real human being, not some sort of phantom of cold-war mythology. Reality, that was it. I wanted to relate to him. I wanted to have a relationship with him. If I could release him from his disguise, perhaps he would even turn into someone I could love. No, surely that was going too far. And yet, I didn't want our relationship to sink to the level of an office affair. That was out of the question. And then another thought occurred to me: what if he was using the machinery of the office for his own purposes? What if he was acting outside the rules, perhaps even of the law? What if he saw my involvement as a threat to himself? What if he had become fearful of me? It was not impossible. Back to the Langhorn case: he must have some plan, an objective. Perhaps that was why he had wanted me out of the way. He was prepared to risk my discovering his identity in order to give himself time to finish the job in my absence.

I slipped on my sandals and walked back to the beach buggy I had been lent. It was time to prepare for the dinner party Laurence Huntington had promised. His parting words at the house had been, 'I want to introduce you tonight to the man who now owns most of Joe Harringay's old petrochemical empire. He's one of my partners in the planned development of Broome.'

When I returned to the guest suite, I discovered that a branch heavy with coconuts had crashed through the tin roof of my bathroom, so I decided to use the shower by the swimming pool. This was situated in a courtyard, around which the house was built.

I reached the side of the pool to find Pat sitting alone sipping a gin and tonic. 'You'd better hurry up,' she said, 'I think Mr Assayd is already here.'

'How do you know?'

'I could hear them talking in the large sitting-room. Your name came up once or twice. I think they must have forgotten that the windows are open. It's very difficult to tell when the mosquito netting is pulled across. You can't hear them now. They must have moved into Laurence's study.'

'Did you pick up anything interesting?' I asked.

'No, but that was probably because most of what they said was drowned out by that radio blaring from the kitchen.'

It certainly would not have been because she had

any trouble hearing. Like her eyesight, the perception of her ears was as acute as it had ever been.

An hour later we sat down to dinner at a rather awkward-sized rectangular oak table. Since there were four of us and the table was sufficiently large to seat at least ten, we were huddled down one end. Laurence Huntington sat at the top of the table. To his left was Mr Assayd. Next to him sat Pat, and I took the place opposite them on Huntington's right. Mrs Huntington did not join us.

We were served throughout by Mr and Mrs Davis, two people of enormous physical proportions and of aboriginal descent, who minded the house for Mr Huntington. Like so many others of their race, they were sullen and rather threatening. Mrs Davis in particular lacked the happy-mamma touch that one associates, for instance, with those in similar circumstances in the southern parts of the United States.

Mr Assayd was the essence of smoothness. Not, I have to say, that I found him particularly attractive. For a start, his balding head was too small for his body and his ears were too big for his head. He had a strong-looking torso, but this appeared to be poorly supported by his short legs, which seemed to bow under the weight they were carrying. Despite all this, he clearly considered himself something of a lady's man. Since I was the only female of the appropriate age present, I became the butt of his leering and winking and consciously risqué humour. I was given no clue, incidentally, as to whether there was a Mrs Assayd.

For all I knew, she was having a ball with Mrs Huntington outside.

'So you were friends of Miss Harringay, excuse me, Mrs Langhorn?' he said soon after the empty oyster shells had been cleared. 'I'm told she was what I believe you English call a bit of a goer in her time. They say she taught Mick Huntington most of what is worth knowing from the Kama-Sutra.'

This time his wink was directed at Laurence, who leered back at the Arab. I let this go. It was in no interest of mine to come to the defence of the late Mrs Langhorn. Maybe it was this lack of response which suddenly triggered a complete change in the tone of his voice. His speech became much slower, less flippant. There was a new sharpness in what he was saying.

'I hope you do not deny your friendship with Mrs Langhorn. What other explanation can there be for the fact that you and Miss Huntington were the only people to attend her funeral?'

'There was one other person,' I said.

His eyes narrowed. 'You are correct. There was one other: a lady, a compatriot of mine.'

'You seem to have taken an extraordinarily close interest in the old lady,' I said.

He took a sip of his wine. His thin lips spread into a smile.

'Are you really surprised, Lady Hildreth?' he asked. 'It is not often that my close business associates, and that is what Mrs Langhorn was, receive the special attention of the British secret service, for that is what you represent.'

The room fell into silence, which was broken by Laurence Huntington scraping back his chair. The light was beginning to fade but I thought I saw Mr Assayd purse his lips and pretend to throw me a kiss.

Then he said, 'Lady Hildreth, I am only a humble maker of chemicals. Much of my know-how I bought when I took over the Harringay enterprises here in Australia. If you are interested in what we do, maybe I should take you round some of our factories. Needless to say, I would be most happy to entertain you as lavishly as your government would permit. I know you have strict rules about these things. Alternatively, if there are matters of politics which you would like to discuss in greater depth, we could do so in even more convivial surroundings.'

Huntington giggled.

'My yacht in the Mediterranean is well equipped with every toy imaginable: water bikes, swimming pool, beautiful stewards and stewardesses. It would give me the greatest pleasure to invite you there to take a short holiday with me.'

The pace of this conversation was fast, but I had been well trained for precisely such circumstances. Without giving any indication of my astonishment at what had been said, not to mention my uncertainty as to where it was all leading, I met him head-on.

'What I think you are saying, Mr Assayd, is that there is some deal you would like to make; something you have to offer and something you would like in return. Have I guessed correctly?'

His smile faded. 'That depends, dear lady, on what you have to offer. The stakes from my point of view are very high indeed. The costs have already been considerable. Mrs Langhorn, for one, paid with her life. That perhaps might have been unnecessary had we been able properly to ascertain whether your government would be willing to enter into discussions. The trouble with the British is that they always pretend to take the high ground in any negotiations; in reality, they are just as willing as the rest of us to do business. It is all very confusing. Often the negotiations never take place and sometimes it leads to mistakes. Perhaps the death of Mrs Langhorn was one of them. It would make it much easier if the British would come off what I think you call their high horse much earlier.'

'Your English is very good,' I said.

He inclined his head. 'That is kind of you. I was at Cambridge University for two years doing a Ph.D. in Chemistry. What is your opinion about a further meeting?'

'I will consult my superiors,' I said.

'And the few days to be spent in the sun on my boat in the Mediterranean?'

'That depends too on what my boss has to say.'

'Ah, the director-general, the "chief," I believe you call him. I know all about your boss. He began his life in this part of Australia too. I am sure you are aware of that, dear Lady Hildreth.'

'Yes, I am aware of it.'

'What did you make of all that?' Pat asked as we crossed the courtyard on our way back to our suite of rooms. I looked down at the kidney-shaped swimming pool sparkling in the artificial light. I considered the idea of taking a quick plunge into it, and then dismissed the thought as being rather childish.

'I can make some intelligent guesses,' I replied, 'but I really haven't a clue.'

'In that case your acting talents have come a long way over the years,' she said. 'What are you going to do?'

'It's time to go and see the chief,' I said decisively. 'For once he will have to meet me on equal terms. Shall I ask him out to lunch? After all, I am still on leave.'

Pat chuckled. 'Don't forget that he's a man. Men have such frightful pride, which can so easily be pricked. Then they deflate like balloons. Go easy on him, Jane.'

I did a skip and a jump like I used to do in hopscotch as a pre-pubescent girl.

'Man or no man, he can't stop me calling him by his name.' I turned round to Pat and made a low bow. 'Good evening, Mr Beverley. Welcome to the real world, where people fall in love and even on occasions bite each other's ears off.'

I clasped her hands and we both laughed. Our laughter could no doubt be heard by the animals in the wildlife park, beyond the electrically controlled front gate and along the road of compressed red dust.

11

'Good evening, Mr Beverley.'

He was less startled than I had expected him to be. In fact, to be honest, he didn't seem to be very startled at all. He rose immediately from where he had been waiting for me in the corner of the restaurant and pulled back a chair at his side.

'I hope you like this pub,' he said. 'I chose it because it's equidistant between our two homes.'

'It's lovely,' I said, 'and thank you for inviting me. The original idea was that you would be my guest.'

He resumed his seat on my right. I knew I was looking pretty good but I wondered whether he had noticed it. The tight white silk dress was cut low; it displayed my shoulders tanned by the Australian sun, which had also lightly bleached my long golden hair. If my looks didn't interest him now, they never would.

'It's the first time I have taken one of my agents

out to dinner,' he said. He added, 'And I'm very nervous about it. I'm not even sure whether it's ethical.'

'That depends on whether or not you are married,' I responded breathlessly.

'I'm not,' he said.

This was moving rather faster than I had anticipated.

'What will you have to drink?' I heard him ask.

'As I'm driving, I'll have a Campari and soda, please, and then just one glass of wine.'

He placed his fingers together as if he were about to pray and then rubbed the insides of his hands down the sides of his nose.

'Do you mind if we take what you discovered about me in Australia as read? May we talk shop instead?'

'By all means, Chief.'

'My Christian name is Adam.'

'I see.' I am sure I must have blushed.

'Let's get that Campari,' he suggested, smiling at the nearest waiter.

Then he turned to face me directly, locking his blue eyes onto mine.

'This Mr Assayd. What do you think he wanted from Mrs Langhorn?'

'Do you mind if I ask you a question first?' He failed to reply and I took this as a signal to continue. 'I hope you won't think it impertinent of me, but I must be quite clear on what terms this conversation is going to proceed. What I am trying to say is that your family was intimately tied up at one point with the Harringays. Your mother, I understand, was probably the mistress of Mrs Langhorn's brother. I have to be clear at least whether your interest in all this is purely personal or whether this is a genuine departmental job. Frankly, I'm happy to play it either way, but I don't think I can cope with muddling the two together.'

The Campari was placed in front of me. 'What are you drinking?' I asked.

'I'll stick to water,' he said. Then he added, 'The answer to your question is a very simple one. This is a departmental job if ever there was one. You must surely have appreciated that yourself by now.'

And that was that: no further confessions, no discussion of why he had wanted to take me off the assignment. Most of the script I had written in my mind for the evening would have to be scrapped.

'So what is it that I am supposed to do now?' I asked in what I later regretfully concluded must have sounded like a rather sulky tone. I was conscious that I was rapidly losing the initiative to him.

He smiled. There was nothing false or contrived about that. His whole body seemed to relax. He leaned back in his chair and let out a deep contented sigh. There was sudden merriment in his eyes. Even their colour seemed to have mellowed. I wanted to move my chair closer to him. I dared not do so. He was my boss. He was also a man for whom I was beginning to feel an immense attraction.

He said, 'Let's be frank, Jane. I would have preferred to have you working around the office on this one, but you're too deeply into it now not to see it through. What started as an innocent practical idea of asking you to pop down the road from your house to do a little preliminary investigation got a bit out of hand.'

'Is that it?' I asked.

The vernacular seemed to puzzle him. 'Is what it?'

'Are those my marching orders?' I had never before spoken to him in such familiar terms. I realized that it was going to be very difficult to go back now. From my point of view at least, it could never be quite the same between us. It might even mean that I would eventually have to find another job.

Then, unexpectedly, for the first time he laughed. 'Of course not. The night, as they say, is still young. We have much more business to complete when, that is, we have finished dinner. By the way, let's order. What are you going to eat?'

I had quails' eggs on a warm salad, followed by Dover sole. He chose smoked salmon and pheasant. We shared half a bottle of Burgeuil rosé. Perhaps in part due to the strength of the Loire wine, we ate for most of the time in comfortable silence. As far as I remember, I felt no compulsion to make conversation: his presence was good enough. He appeared equally content. It was an immensely satisfying feeling that he seemed to be enjoying himself. Not entirely, I confess, for the first time, I wondered what was the difference in our ages. My guess was that he was about ten years older than me.

It is possible, of course, that my memory is playing tricks with me, that we talked more than I now recollect. In that case, the sheer force of his presence trivialized whatever it was that we said to each other.

I do remember that at some point in between the courses he said, 'It was clever of you to play along with Assayd's belief that you had come to negotiate with him. That could be very helpful. It is one reason, of course, why you must now pursue this case.'

In the far corner of the room a log burned slowly in a Tudor-style fireplace. At last, too soon, a waiter emerged to clear away our empty plates.

'Do you mind if we skip coffee?' the chief said.

'Are you in a hurry to get away?' I fear there might have been a slight whine in my voice.

'There is an awful lot to do,' he replied.

'I haven't enjoyed a dinner so much for a very long time,' I said.

'I'm very flattered,' he said. Then he rose briskly from his seat. Standing behind me, he prepared to pull back my chair. Had his movement been less decisive, I might have made one more attempt to persuade him to linger a little longer. As it was, I stood up myself and allowed him to guide me towards the door. As we moved through the tables, I was aware of the attention we were attracting from the other guests. Although he was tall and I am rather petite, our movement together seemed to have a rhythm which I still cannot fully explain. I wanted him to put his arm around my shoulders, but this I knew was hoping for too much.

Outside the dining-room, in the reception area, I received my first real surprise of the evening. Leaning over the reception desk engrossed in intimate conversation with a middle-aged blonde lady who kept patting the back of her hair was the chief's driver, Bert. When he saw me he grinned. 'Hello, there,' he said in broad cockney.

I turned round to my boss. 'I thought you had driven yourself,' I said.

'I did,' he replied. 'Bert has been brought over to take your car back to Chipping Campden. Unless you object, you're coming with me.'

'I see,' I said. 'But why all the mystery? Couldn't we have discussed this over dinner?' It was the first time I had ever questioned his judgement.

'Because dining-rooms in smart restaurants are not the most secure of places in which to discuss the kinds of topics which we will have to deal with tonight.'

I was conscious that Bert was winking at me. 'Any special quirks in your motor, Lady H?' he asked.

'Not that I can think of, Bert. How will you get back after you've dumped my car?'

'Ah, well, there you are. The great office in the sky has thought of everything. I've got an escort car, haven't I, the one that brought me here. I'm to deliver your Merc into the safe hands of Miss Huntington, then me mate Jack will spirit me back to London quicker than you can say "Flash Gordon." Isn't that right, sir?'

'If that's what you and Miss Fry sorted out,' the chief said stiffly.

'To the letter, sir, or rather, to the word.'

Of the two, the word was of greater meaning to Bert since he was almost illiterate: certainly joined-up writing was beyond him.

'Okay, let's get on with it,' the chief ordered.

'Will you be wanting me tomorrow morning, sir?' Bert asked.

'Yes, please. Pick me up off the eight-o'clock train at Paddington, would you.'

A momentary look of disappointment crossed Bert's normally cheerful pug-like face.

'Very good, sir. Usual place by platform ten. I'll park up as close to the concourse as I can.'

'Thank you, Bert. Come on, Jane. We've got a big night ahead of us.'

'Oh, one more thing, sir. Miss Fry told me to tell you that the police had laid everything on. She said you would know what that meant.'

The chief, I discovered for the first time, drove a black Jaguar XJ12, whose speedometer registered a maximum of 160 miles per hour.

'Clumsy car to drive this, very heavy,' he said as we pulled out of a short drive and began to head west along the A40. 'I'm afraid it's had to be made bullet-proof.'

'May I be allowed to know now where we are going?' I asked.

'Of course.' The tone of his voice was strangely matter-of-fact. 'Studwell Manor, where else?'

'Good God,' I said.

'You sound disappointed.' He was smiling.

'I suppose I am. I thought perhaps I was about to be introduced to Château Beverley. It can't be very far away.'

It was beginning to rain and he switched on the windscreen wipers. He began to stare intensely at the road ahead.

After a moment or two he said, 'I do assure you that had I been taking you to my home, I would not have done so without your prior knowledge and permission.'

'I understand,' I said, rather chastened. After this we drove in silence. I couldn't help notice the frequency with which he looked in his mirror, despite the emptiness of the road. When we were about five miles away from Studwell, he seemed to relax.

Suddenly he said, 'The vehicle behind us is a police car. I've been expecting it. Don't be surprised at the protection which has been thrown around the Manor.'

As if to confirm what he had just said, the gates when we approached the drive were firmly closed. The chief flashed his headlights four times. This seemed to be the signal for one of the gates to open. Two men in civilian clothes stepped out in front of our car. The chief lowered his window and showed them his ID card, which he had withdrawn from the inside pocket of his suit jacket.

One of the men said, 'Very good, sir. I'll open the other gate.'

As soon as we were in the drive, the house became bathed in floodlights. The chief stopped the car and opened his door. He called back to the men at the gates, 'Is Sergeant Braniff around, do you know?'

I could not hear their answer but it must have been affirmative because the chief said, 'In the house, is he? Okay, I'll find him.'

He drove up to the front door, then he said, 'This is it, Jane. Let's go inside.'

He pressed the bell beside the front door, which was immediately opened by a young policeman in uniform.

'Is Sergeant Braniff around?'

'Yes, sir. He's expecting you. I think he's in what was the dining-room.'

We crossed the hall, which was completely empty, stripped of all the paraphernalia which had been littered around it on my last visit. As we reached the dining-room, a man in his twenties emerged to greet us. He was wearing a white open-necked shirt and no tie.

'Good evening, sir. Good evening, Lady Hildreth.' His voice was very precise and youthful. 'Do you want to go straight over, sir?'

'I think so, don't you? No point in delaying.'

'Follow me then, if you will, sir.'

He led the way to the back of the hall, down a short passage and out into the garden. The lawns were white and unreal in the floodlights. The flower-beds had been tidied and the yew hedges cut. It was all hardly recognizable as the place I had walked through barely two weeks earlier. The young man led us down a gravel path towards the swimming pool. We made straight for the changing-rooms on the far side. Our companion took out a bunch of keys and began to unlock with one of them a padlock fixed to the changing-room door. Once inside, he turned on a light. The room was empty.

'It's over there,' he said, pointing to the far corner.

At first I was uncertain what it was that we were meant to be looking at. Then I saw it: a wooden trap-door.

'The opening was covered in carpeting when it was found,' the man said. 'There is no one down there at the moment. Do you want to take a look for yourself?'

'That's the general idea, Sergeant,' the chief said.

The policeman looked at me. 'Will you be all right in that tight skirt, miss? You'll have to go down a step-ladder.'

'I've done worse things in my life,' I said. 'But perhaps I ought to go down first.'

He blushed, rather sweetly, I thought. Then he laughed and said, 'I think I had better lead the way. I promise not to look up. It's all a bit complicated down there. Here goes.'

He lifted the trapdoor and turned a switch under the floor. Then he swung his legs over the edge and disappeared down the hole. I followed him. The chief came down after me.

As my foot touched the ground, the policeman said, 'Whoever they were who were operating this outfit were burrowed down here like moles.'

I began to look around me. What I saw was a long low bunker some twenty metres in length and about three metres high. The walls were lined with shelves laden with bottles full of coloured liquids and powders. Below the shelves on the right-hand side there was a bench which extended along the entire length of the room. On the left there was ranged what looked like a row of refrigerators.

'Were we given a tip-off about this?' I asked the chief.

'Not exactly. A friendly organization advised us that if we searched hard enough, we were likely to come up with something of interest. The person who actually found it was a member of the local force. To be strictly accurate, his dog sniffed it out. The door we came through above us was actually rather well disguised with imitation concrete.'

'Is it what it appears to be?' I asked.

'That depends on what you think it is,' the chief replied. 'Sergeant Braniff here is a police chemist and he will explain.'

'If you step this way, Lady Jane, I can point out some of the chemical features. Much of it is pretty straightforward. This container over here contains hydrogen cyanide. That can be pretty nasty stuff. If it enters the body through the lungs, it kills the victim by preventing oxygen from reaching the bloodstream. There are even more potent substances in here.'

He pressed a series of buttons on a panel beside one of the fridges. The door swung open, revealing a series of racks behind a steel grille.

'You can't see them very clearly,' the policeman said, 'but the caskets on those shelves contain several different nerve agents, like sarin, soman and tabun. Saddam Hussein used a mixture of mustard gas, sarin and tabun to kill five thousand Kurds a few years ago. They cause, among other things, lung congestion. Also in there is phosgene, which fills the lungs with liquid and can be pretty lethal. In the next cabinet, which for obvious reasons I won't open, there are molecules of anthrax, cholera, typhoid and botulism.'

'Suddenly it feels rather cold in here,' I said.

'Horrible stuff, this,' the sergeant went on, 'but sadly pretty commonplace these days in certain parts of the world. What makes this place really interesting is over here on the open shelves.'

He pointed to one of the small cans sitting on a shelf just above my head. 'This is difluro and this is isopropyl alcohol amine. On their own they are fairly harmless substances. We have reason to believe that they were experimenting here with the technology of mixing the two together. When that happens, a really lethal nerve agent is created.'

'What would happen,' the chief intervened, 'is that the two chemicals would be placed separately in a container, say the tip of a missile. When the container struck its target, the barrier between the two would collapse, allowing them to mix. The trick, if it were a shell or a missile, would be to make it burst between fifty and two hundred feet above the ground so that the filthy stuff would be blown over a very wide area.'

'And this was all Mrs Langhorn's baby,' I said.

The chief scraped the ground with the toe of his shoe. 'So it would seem,' he said. 'I wanted you to see it before the boys started to clean it up tomorrow.'

'Anything more you want from me, sir?'' the policeman asked.

'No. I think that's about it for the moment. I'll take Lady Hildreth home now. If necessary, I will liaise again with you through our Special Branch people.'

'Very good, sir. If you and Lady Jane would like to go on up, I'll just make sure everything is shipshape here before I follow you. The armed guards who are dotted about around the bushes should know who you are.'

A few minutes later, I sat beside the chief in his car. We were driving north towards Chipping Campden.

'That was all laboratory stuff, of course,' he said.

'What we have got to discover is whether any of it was manufactured and delivered in usable form.'

The road rose steeply into the Cotswolds. On either side, tall black conifers blotted out the skyline.

'Mr Assayd?' I asked.

'He's certainly worth a try, especially if he believes he has something to negotiate from us.'

'So I accept his invitation to join him on his yacht?'

'Can you cope with him?' he asked.

'I sincerely hope so,' I replied.

'What will you do if he tries to overpower you?'

'Sexually, you mean?'

For a moment the chief was silent. Then he said quietly, 'I suppose I did mean that.'

'I'll have to cross that bridge when I come to it,' I replied.

He raised his left hand from the gear lever and touched my arm.

'We will do our best to make sure you are protected.'

We were both sufficiently experienced to understand that this meant no more and no less than what he had said.

12

I was met at Nice airport by a man wearing crisp white trousers and a shirt with one button undone at the collar. The gold braid on his epaulettes was that of a naval officer. He held a large piece of white paper over his head; on it were printed the words *'Pacific Queen.'* Underneath, in blue-ink capital letters, was written my name.

'Where is she berthed?' I asked him as we walked towards the exit to the terminal building.

'Antibes,' he said. 'Not many other ports around here will take a ship of her size.'

'How big is she?'

'Three thousand tonnes. She's not the newest boat in the Med, but she's one of the largest and most luxurious. I've been with her since she was launched eight years ago. I'm the second officer, by the way. My name's Paul, Paul Evans.'

'And the rest of the crew, Paul? Have they been with her as long as you?'

'No, the others are pretty new. The present skipper joined us only three weeks ago. He's a close friend of the owner, I believe.'

'Mr Assayd?'

'Yes.'

'I imagine you haven't had much of a chance to get to know Mr Assayd yet?'

'No, you're right. He only bought the boat a few months ago and he's been away for most of the time since then. The previous owner was a businessman from the Midlands. He didn't use the boat much either, but at least he used to charter it out a lot. So we were kept busy in the Med in the summer and in the Caribbean in the winter. It seems that the present owner doesn't plan on doing much chartering.'

We had reached the airport car-park. He led the way to a white Lotus Elan.

'What a nice car,' I said.

'It belongs to the ship. A bit stubby for my liking. Still, you can't have everything.'

He lifted my bag into the boat and held the passenger door open for me. Then he leaped over the driver's door into the bucket seat beside me.

'Do you like the roof up or down? The sun is setting, so it shouldn't be too hot.'

'Down.'

'Down it will be. Depending on the traffic, it should only take us half an hour to the port.'

As Mr Evans had anticipated, the sun began to set

out to sea to our left in a hazy orange ball as we drove west along the coast. Out-of-season holiday-makers were packing beach bags and moving off the pebble beach which stretches most of the way between Nice and Antibes. To our right the hills of the Alpes-Maritimes were fading into their evening colours of mauve and blue. As we approached the outskirts of Antibes, the traffic almost came to a halt.

'Bloody rush-hour,' Paul Evans shouted and switched on the car radio. The heavy beat of Radio Monte Carlo made further conversation impossible. Ten minutes later he turned down the music to say, 'See the port over to the left? If you knew what you were looking for, you could pick out our communications antenna amongst the masts. It's a white dome-shaped object which sticks up rather higher than most of the other ones around.'

I am no expert on private yachts. All I can say is that I was greatly impressed by the one behind whose stern we finally drew up. She was conventionally designed with four decks. Along the main deck were the large square windows of the staterooms. Above them the sleek sloping glass of the bridge was backed by another long row of windows.

By the time I was walking up her gangplank, I had learned from Paul Evans that she had a permanent crew of ten, including a chef who had recently been acquired from Maxim's in Paris. She also carried two motor launches. She had three suites of guest cabins as well as countless single cabins, each with its own bathroom. She had a cinema, library, swimming pool and no doubt much else.

At the top of the gangplank I was met by another naval officer. He was not quite as good-looking as Paul, but he had an aura of greater authority about him. He wore sunglasses and spoke rather softly.

'Welcome aboard the *Pacific Queen*, Lady Hildreth. One of my stewardesses will show you to your rooms. When you are sufficiently refreshed, Mr Assayd will greet you in the main saloon, which is on the top deck immediately behind the bridge. I'm afraid we have a no-shoes rule on deck. I hope this will not inconvenience you too much.'

The stewardess who showed me to my cabin was very pretty, with blonde hair and a light tan. She wore a smart blue skirt and a white short-sleeved blouse. Like the two men, she had epaulettes, in her case crossed by two black stripes.

The walls of my cabin were lined with deepbrown mahogany, as, indeed, had been the corridors and passages which led to it. The suite comprised a bedroom dominated by a double bed, a small sitting-room, and a rather larger bathroom. The latter was decorated in art-deco style and included two aspidistras, which gave the whole thing a tropical look.

'Is there anything you want ironed for dinner?' the girl asked in a slightly Nordic accent.

'Is dinner very formal?' I asked.

'Ladies usually wear a cocktail dress,' she said.

There was a knock at the door.

A voice from outside said, 'Your suitcase, your ladyship.' I called out, 'Do come in,' and to the girl said, 'I would be grateful to have a dress pressed.'

Three quarters of an hour later, just after seven o'clock, I made my entrance into the main saloon in a short green silk cocktail dress. As I did so, Mr Assayd rose from a sofa which faced a wide fireplace. A lady with long blonde hair and a tight black dress remained sitting down.

'Ah, my dear Lady Hildreth. You are very welcome. Anita here was just going, so this is excellent timing.'

With what seemed to me less than perfect grace the girl rose from the sofa where she had been sitting beside Assayd. She looked at her watch and without comment wriggled her way towards the door.

Mr Assayd seemed impervious to this behavior, 'What about a glass of pink champagne?' he inquired.

'That would be nice,' I replied, I'm sure rather stiffly.

He pressed a bell. Almost instantly the door through which his erstwhile companion had just departed reopened. A stewardess, as pretty as the one I had first met but this time with long black hair, entered carrying the champagne on a silver tray.

'Chef presents his compliments, sir, and asks whether it will be convenient to dine at eight o'clock.'

'That will be fine,' my host replied.

'Will there be other guests tonight?' she asked.

'No, Lady Hildreth and I will dine alone. If Mr Huntington shows up from Australia, he can join us tomorrow.' He added, I think for my benefit, 'That's Laurence Huntington, of course.'

The stewardess poured the frothy pink liquid into two very finely cut tulip-shaped glasses. Assayd pointed one of these to his nose and commented, 'That will do.' Then he raised the glass in my direction and said, 'To our future co-operation.'

'We have much to discuss, Mr Assayd,' I agreed.

'Come and sit beside me,' he said, pointing at the position on the sofa recently vacated by the girl in the black skirt. 'I am much looking forward to making your acquaintance. May I call you Jane? My first name is Hisham.'

I had no real alternative but to sit down where he had suggested. Nor could I think of any real objection to the swapping of our given names. He placed himself rather closer to me than I would have chosen and stretched his right arm behind me along the back of the settee.

'Do you like music?' he asked.

'Yes,' I said.

'What sort?'

'Mozart, Brahms, Elgar,' I answered somewhat wildly.

'You shall have them all,' he said, pressing a bell on the floor with the tip of a black Gucci shoe. The stewardess with the black hair re-emerged.

'Mozart concertos,' he ordered.

Within seconds the room was filled with the resonant chords of the First Allegro.

He straightened the lapels of a deep-blue jacket which he wore over a silk polo-necked shirt. Then he passed his left hand over his balding head.

'Where shall we start?' I asked.

He screwed up his narrow eyes and sighed. 'Not too fast, my dear Jane, not too fast.'

Removing his right arm from behind my back, he placed his hand on my left elbow. I concentrated hard on not withdrawing it.

'We must get to know each other first. There is no need to rush. We have the whole night ahead and tomorrow we can lie on deck in the sun talking to each other as much as we wish. Please have some more champagne. It's excellent, don't you think. I buy it direct from the vineyard.'

'You manufacture chemicals?' I persisted.

'That is a substantial part of my business,' he agreed.

'Do you make your products according to formulae supplied by the late Mrs Langhorn?'

'That is a direct and very difficult question to answer,' he said. 'Let us chew on it, as they say, over dinner. The dining-room is one deck down at the stern of the boat. Shall we go?'

I followed him out of the saloon onto the deck outside. Beside us another yacht, not quite as grand as the one we were on, rode gently at anchor, silent and deserted. In the middle distance beyond, we could see the lights of the cafés in the tourist part of the town. A hum of human and mechanical noise echoed towards us from across the harbour. Every so often this was punctuated by the screech of a car horn, itself to be drowned out by the hubbub of laughter and shouting. On the quay to the stern of the boat, two old men staggered past with bottles held up to their lips. Beneath their feet, a gang of children sat gossiping like tiny moths under the beam of an old street light.

We climbed down a flight of stairs and walked aft. We entered the dining saloon through an anteroom at the stern. Two places had been laid out at the end of a large mahogany table. The only light in the room came from candles placed in holders around the wall and from a small spotlight in the ceiling which illuminated a bowl of rose petals in the centre of the table. The two stewardesses stood side by side at the far end of the room. As we approached the table, each took hold of what looked like a genuine Hepplewhite chair and pulled it out.

'Please bring some more of that champagne,' Assayd ordered, 'and have the music piped through here.'

The top of his head glistened in the candlelight. Despite the air-conditioning, he seemed to be sweating.

When we were seated, he at the end of the table and I to his right, he leaned towards me.

'You are very beautiful,' he said. 'I thought so

from the first time I saw you. I hope we shall be very close friends.'

I refrained from saying, 'Like the girl you kicked out when I arrived.' Instead, I replied, 'That rather depends on what business we are able to complete together.'

His smile pulled his face back into the shape of a frog. 'You are also very mercenary. I like that.'

' "Mercenary" implies that money is to be transacted.'

'Is that what you want?' he asked quickly.

'What do you think, Mr Assayd?'

He sipped from his glass and eyed me simultaneously.

'Lady Jane, I will be very frank with you. I wish to make love to you and within reason I will do what it takes to secure your compliance. I should add that I have certain information which you require and you have certain favours which you can give.'

'And that is the basis of the deal you spoke of in Broome?' I asked him.

He did not reply.

'I am disappointed. I had expected—how shall I put it?—something more important from you.'

He stared at me for a moment in silence. His perfume—aftershave would have been a misnomer—smelt of incense, sweet and sickly.

Then he said, 'You provide me with a challenge and I accept. I must prove to you that I matter, that I am someone fit to do business with a representative of Her Majesty's government. I am very happy with this challenge. Nothing that is interesting comes too easily. Let us eat. I hope that you like caviar and lobster bouillabaisse because that is what I have ordered.' He clapped his hands. 'We will start,' he shouted to the blonde stewardess. Her bare feet drummed against the deck as she hurried to carry out the command.

He turned to me again. 'It is easier this way,' he said. 'I need not so much to win your confidence as to impress you. Let me then offer you a sample of what I can contribute. Let us talk of Dr John Swinton.'

For a moment my mind went blank. I hoped I did not show it.

'It was you, I believe, Lady Jane, who first discovered his body suspended from an oak tree in the village of Studwell?'

'Chestnut tree,' I said. 'If we're talking about Jack Swinton, I found him hanging from a chestnut tree.'

'I will not argue that point with you. If you say it was a chestnut tree, it was a chestnut tree. Nor, I suspect, will you wish to dispute with me the importance of the research Dr Swinton was able to conduct on our behalf into various advances in biological weaponry. I know that your people have found the laboratory at Studwell Manor. As far as Dr Swinton himself is concerned, I think we can admire not only his formidable mind as a chemist, but also his mastery of the art of presenting himself to the local people as a village idiot. It is true, of course, that without the

Langhorn wealth and network he would never have managed to pursue his interests as effectively as was the case. But he was in his way a great man, don't you think?'

'Until in the end he and the Langhorns knew too much?' It was a guess, but in the circumstances not too wide a one.

He lowered his eyes. 'You must not press me too hard, Jane. Not, that is, unless you are willing to come up with your side of the bargain.'

'You must give me time to think about it,' I said. 'It may even be necessary for me to return home for a few days to consider the implications of what you have just said.'

He shrugged. 'I can wait for a few days. After a while, however, I may lose interest. Then we could both be the losers.'

I smiled at him. 'Let's relax and enjoy this lovely meal,' I suggested.

Later that night, with my cabin door firmly bolted, I called the chief on my radio transmitter.

'Strangely enough,' I said, 'I don't think the real point of this is to get me into bed with him.'

'I hope you're right,' came the crackling reply.

'From his point of view, it might be a bonus. My antennae tell me he's really on to something more important. If I'm wrong, the whole thing takes on the characteristics of a farce, don't you think?'

There was a definite pause before he answered, 'Farce or not, I would keep your gun handy. Somehow I will arrange to have you taken off the boat tomorrow. You'll need to tell Assayd that you wish to confer with your superiors. Incidentally, I don't think this is likely to turn out to be a farce. What you have just told me confirms one or two pieces of intelligence we have been picking up at this end.'

13

When I came out on deck the next morning, we were anchored off a long white sandy beach. The sea was calm and patched with blues and greens.

'Tahiti Plage, Saint-Tropez,' a friendly voice said from my right. 'The owner likes to spot the beautiful naturists through his telescope. Not that in my opinion the fat ones make much of a sight in their birthday suits.'

'Good morning, Paul,' I said. 'I am afraid I overslept. How long were we sailing for?' He pushed his white-peaked cap to the back of his bronzed, open face. 'About three quarters of an hour. We set a straight course along the coast.'

'Is Mr Assayd up and about yet?' I asked.

'He's sunning himself on the top deck. I am sure he would be delighted to see you. He's not used to being on his own, not at least when he's on the boat.'

When I reached him, Assayd was lying on his front dressed only in a red G-string. The stewardess with the dark hair was crouched over him massaging the top of his back.

'I can ask one of the male crew to give you a massage if you would like it,' he said.

'I don't think I could take the pressure,' I lied. I was trained to bear the strain of a two-hundred-pound weight on my back.

'Besides,' I added, 'I am leaving to confer with my colleagues.'

He rolled over and waved the stewardess away.

'I know,' he said. 'We intercepted your radio conversation. You are right, Lady Jane, there is more I want from you than your body, though that would have been nice too. If I am perfectly frank, there are more fish in the sea, or rather, fifty metres across the sea from where we are anchored.' He stood up and surveyed the distant beach. 'Look at them all, the lovely creatures. If I were speaking for myself alone, maybe a night of passion with you would indeed have satisfied me, but the truth, as you or your people have suspected, is that I do not act for myself alone. Like you, I work for a cause: to be more precise, for a nation. My chemical plants in Australia make me a good deal of money and I enjoy myself with what I have earned, but there is more to life than the accumulation of riches. I have principles, Lady Jane, as I am sure you have, grand designs. That is why I am able to be ruthless, not only against my enemies but against anyone who for no fault of his own stands in my way.

I know you to be an intelligent woman. I am sure you understand what I am saying.'

He was interrupted by a shout from the deck below.

The voice said, 'Yes, we do have Lady Hildreth on board. Who shall I say wishes to speak to her?'

A moment later, Paul Evans appeared on the sun deck. He spoke to Assayd.

'A Sunseeker high-speed cruiser has just pulled alongside, sir. I know her skipper. He hangs around the clubhouse in Antibes. He says he has been commissioned to collect Lady Hildreth.'

Assayd looked at me. 'Do you wish to go in this way?' he asked. 'If you would prefer it, I will arrange for a fast boat from the *Pacific Queen* to take you to the port which is most convenient for you.'

With my left elbow I adjusted the hand gun strapped inside my blouse. Then I said, 'I'll go now. My bag is packed and waiting in my cabin.'

'Very well,' the Arab replied. 'I assume you will return swiftly. We have hardly begun our discussions. I will wait for you here for four days. After that I will leave and it will be too late. I think your people understand enough now of what is going on to see that there are matters of great international concern at stake.'

He lay back on his mattress. There was no question of his accompanying me to the side of the boat. So I was quite alone as I descended the steps to the motor launch which was rolling alongside. I paused on a small platform at the foot of the ladder and looked up to the deck above me. Paul Evans managed a slight, coy, wave.

As I jumped onto the foredeck of the waiting craft, a short man with close-cropped hair and wearing white jeans stepped up to help me. His bare chest was strangely white and hairless.

'The name's Luke,' he said in a South African accent. 'Welcome aboard. We're modern and very fast but not as big as where you have just come from.'

He guided me towards the cockpit of the boat. 'I suggest you sit down, madam. When we get going, it will feel as if we are taking off. If you're interested in these things, we build up rapidly to thirty knots. As a matter of fact, we're the fastest turbine vessel of its kind afloat. Anything faster works on water jets.'

I was glad that I took his advice as the bow of the boat began to rise and the vessel jerked into life. Screened by spray on either side, we headed straight out to sea. Within minutes we were out of sight of the beach. As soon as the communications antenna on the *Pacific Queen* had disappeared, my new skipper pulled back the throttle and the bow of the boat sank back into the water.

'What's the problem?' I asked.

'No problem, madam. I must, however, ask you to go down into the cabin.'

'Is that necessary?' I demanded, suddenly tensing.

'I fear so.'

I withdrew my gun from inside my shirt and pointed it at him.

The door of the cabin crashed open and the chief stood in its entrance. He was smiling.

'That's a bit melodramatic, isn't it, Jane?' he said.

'If we're talking about melodrama . . .' I was interrupted by the package he tossed at me. It fell noiselessly at my feet.

'Several female bathing costumes of the very latest design,' he said. 'I'm going for a swim. You're very welcome to join me.'

As he emerged fully into the open cockpit, he looked sleek and tanned. His faded brown-patterned swimming shorts came almost to his knees. They suited him.

'You'll find all the changing facilities you need downstairs,' Luke said.

When I reached the bottom of the steps I saw what he meant. Although designed as a speed boat, its cabin space was air-conditioned and beautifully appointed with thick carpets and furnishings in pastel shades. A door to the left led into a very modern bathroom.

The plastic bag which the chief had thrown to me contained two one-piece swimsuits and a bikini. Each fitted me perfectly; the person who had bought them knew my exact measurements. I decided against the bikini and chose the one in luminous pink and black. It was extremely well cut, if perhaps a little daringly in the bottom. I imagine it had cost a lot of money.

When I came back on deck, Luke gave a low whistle.

'Your boss has disappeared,' he said. 'Swum out of sight. Christ, he's a strong swimmer. I've never seen anything like it. You should see how long he can stay under water.'

I went to the stern of the boat and dived off a small platform above one of the two propellors. I too am a strong swimmer and began to crawl, no doubt at some speed, away from the boat. I had been in the water for about five minutes when suddenly he sur-faced in front of me. Goodness knows where he had come from.

'Nice to know I can still play the old tricks we learned in the service,' he said. I assumed by 'service' he meant the SAS. 'I remember that one was particu-larly useful when we were told to get out of Aden, as it then was, without the use of boats.'

'How long can you stay under water?' I shouted.

'I've never timed myself.'

I changed the subject. 'What are we doing here?'

'Having fun.'

'At the taxpayer's expense?'

'I assure you, Jane, he'll get value for his money later in the day.'

Some time later I clambered up the ladder which Luke had thoughtfully lowered at the stern of the boat.

'There's a nozzle at the side which you can pull

out for a shower. It even does hot water if you want it.' The chief's voice seemed very close behind me.

'Who does this belong to?' I asked.

'What?'

'This gorgeous boat.'

'Me,' he said simply. 'I used to keep a sailing boat down here. The problem was she was too large for me to handle on my own. It became rather too much of a sweat recruiting a crew whenever I wanted to use her. This is a compromise. I can skipper her myself if I want, or if I'm busy, as we will be today, I can get people like Luke to help.'

'When do we start being busy?' I asked.

'As soon as we have had some lunch.'

When I reached the cockpit I found that Luke had laid out an exotic-looking salad Niçoise.

'I would like to reach Monte Carlo at about three o'clock,' the chief said to Luke. 'That means leaving here in about half an hour.'

After lunch I lay out on the deck at the stern. The sun beat down on my back but I didn't feel its heat. I was cooled by the rush of the wind and by the spray as we roared eastwards towards the principality of Monaco. Through my half-closed eyes, I could just make out the misty contours of the mountains along the coastline. Sitting behind me, panama hat on his head, blue denim shirt unbottoned at the neck, horn-rimmed dark glasses firmly perched on his aristocratic nose, every inch the British gentleman, I could feel the presence of my boss. He was reading that morning's *Nice Matin*. It occurred to me for the first time that I might be falling in love with him.

14

Luke edged the bow of the Sunseeker past the lighthouse on our port side and around the glass-fronted control office on the starboard. Then he turned the boat sharp right and reversed engines. We came smoothly to a halt beside an empty quay. Above and behind us loomed the ornate frontage of the palace. To our front were the casino and the Hôtel de Paris. We clambered out of the cockpit and jumped over the railings onto land. As we began to walk briskly round the harbour, Luke pulled the boat away.

'I'll be on the other side of the harbour wall when you want me,' he called.

After two or three minutes, the chief turned right, away from the water's edge. We went through a door and headed towards a lift.

'This will bring us out just below the casino,' he said. 'From there it's only a very short walk to the Hôtel de Paris.'

The antiques fair in the exhibition centre of the

hotel was, in the words of the chief, "not for the faint-hearted." The entrance fee alone was one hundred francs a head. We climbed a marble staircase to the first floor, where twenty or so booths displayed some of the world's most fabulous artefacts. The chief wove his way unhesitatingly to stand number 19. Here were laid out some of the smaller works of Rembrandt and Pieter Brueghel.

'I suppose it's a sign of these recessionary times that they have paintings of this quality to sell at all,' he muttered.

Approaching a young man in an immaculately cut and pressed light-grey suit, he asked, 'Is Mr Sayff about?'

The young man bowed rather quaintly almost down to his waist and then asked in French-accented English, 'Who shall I tell Mr Sayff it is who wishes to see him?' Presumably he thought himself to be in the presence of an enormously important buyer.

'Mr Donaldson,' the chief lied. At least, I assumed it was a lie.

Another deep bow. 'Perhaps you and your lady will be so kind as to sit down for a moment.' He pointed to several gilt chairs.

'Don't worry,' the chief said. 'We'll wait here. I imagine Mr Sayff won't be too long.'

'I will go and find him.' The young man disappeared through a door at the back of the stand; thirty seconds later he re-emerged accompanied by a portly gentleman with grey skin and a moustache which drooped almost to the lower edge of his chin. He wore a white robe and came straight up to us.

'Mr Donaldson? I am very glad to see you. This must be Lady Hildreth. You are both very welcome. It is most good of you to come so promptly. Thank you, Jacques. I will take care of our guests from here.' He spoke English with a faultless upper-class accent.

The young man backed away as if we were royalty.

Mr Sayff dropped his voice to a whisper. 'As I am sure you understand, we cannot talk here. Strangely enough, the securest place around here is the ice-cream restaurant in the square outside. If you have no objection, I will meet you there in about five minutes. I hope you both like ice cream.' The inference was that Mr Sayff did.

The five minutes turned into fifteen and I could sense the chief's growing restlessness. For the third time, he said to a pretty waitress dressed in a chic pink-and-white uniform, '*Pardon, mademoiselle. Nous attendons un ami.*' His accent sounded impeccable.

To me he muttered. 'I'm sure she thinks we're here for a free sit-down away from the sun. What on earth can have happened to the man? After all, the whole exercise has been his idea from the start.'

We were about to return to the exhibition hall when he arrived, pouring with sweat and evidently out of breath.

'A thousand apologies,' he said. 'Just after you left, a genuine buyer emerged. Even we are interested in genuine buyers.'

'Did you sell?' the chief asked, with obvious indifference to the answer.

The Arab waved his head slowly from side to side. 'That we will not be able to tell for several days. The main problem will be checking the man's credentials. We know nothing about him. At our end of the business, that is very unusual. Typically a buyer and a seller of a Rembrandt have been sniffing around each other for weeks. With a new buyer it is very exceptional also for there to be no agent involved. Of course, we know all the important agents throughout the world. But you haven't come here to talk about art. Let me get the ice creams first.' He flicked his fingers at one of the waitresses in a manner which few Westerners would dare.

Without consulting us, he ordered four '*glaces avec chocolat et noix.*'

'Now, my dear friend,' he said, turning to the chief, 'this is very good of you. I am most impressed by the efficiency of the British intelligence service and so, I have no doubt, will be His Royal Highness.'

'Prince El-Mummed?' the chief inquired.

'You are well informed, my friend. I would have expected no less.'

'It was not too difficult,' my boss replied. 'After all, we knew that it was someone who had recently resigned from the government.'

'Quite so.'

Then Mr Sayff turned to me and said, 'You have just come from the yacht belonging to Hisham Assayd?'

'That is correct.'

At this point the waitress deposited four sickly-looking ice creams in front of each of us. Judging by the sparkle which made its sudden appearance in his otherwise cold grey eyes, the arrival of the ice cream gave our host some satisfaction.

'A dangerous man,' he muttered.

'Assayd?' I asked.

'A very dangerous man. Whether or not he is evil will depend upon what perspective you are viewing him from. From my point of view it is sufficient to know that he is an enemy.'

He lifted a large dollop of white ice cream to his mouth. His thick lips seemed to search for it like the tentacle tips of an octopus. With his mouth still full, he mumbled, 'I know what he wants from you.'

I wondered for a moment whether he was mocking me. This thought was soon dispelled by what he said next.

'The government of my country supports him in his desires.'

'But His Highness does not?' the chief intervened.

'Precisely.'

'And you act for His Highness, even though he has resigned from the government?'

For a moment there was no response. Then Mr

Sayff rocked back on his chair and laughed. He slapped the chief on the back with a vigour that would have inflicted an injury on many men. The chief merely continued to watch him without showing any obvious emotion.

'I may be a lover of ice cream,' he roared, 'but I am also a man of honour. His Highness is my protector and my leader. It will not be long before he returns to power, especially if you are able to help him.'

'I believe he has a mansion somewhere on the coast here. Is that where you plan that we should meet?' the chief asked.

Mr Sayff shook his head. A dribble of chocolated saliva flowed from the corner of his mouth.

'He is in Jedda, and for the present he intends to remain there. He does not think it would be safe at the moment to leave his home.'

'So he wants us to go to Jedda?'

Again he shook his head. This time it was the wobble of his thick jowls which attracted my attention.

'It is Lady Hildreth who has had the direct contact with Assayd and it is she whom His Highness wishes to meet, alone. He understands that she will be operating entirely to your orders. He wishes, nevertheless, to deal through her.'

Sayff looked at me directly. His eyes had a squint which I had not noticed before. Then he grinned and added, 'Maybe it is because he has had a chance to study her photographs.'

'In that case we will hold His Highness directly responsible for her safety.' There was an unwonted intensity in the chief's voice. I thought I even detected a blush of colour on his left cheek, but that might well have been a trick of the setting sun.

'I will escort her to Saudi Arabia personally on the private jet,' the Arab replied.

Apparently not wholly satisfied with this offer, the Chief capped it with one of his own. 'And I will have some of my people very close by.'

I have to say this sounded more like a threat than a friendly contribution to general resources.

Mr Sayff rose from the table.

'When will you be ready to go?' he asked me.

'As soon as you wish,' I said.

'Then let us depart this evening from Nice Airport. I will meet you in the VIP suite in two hours' time, at eight-thirty.' He turned to the chief. 'It is good of your government to have been so co-operative. I hope we shall be able to repay you in some way.'

He looked down at the table. His ice cream was no more. Ours had melted into little pools of mud-coloured liquid.

'You don't like ice cream,' he said. 'At least you do not have to foot the bill for it. It will be sent with all the others to my office. I think it may be cheaper to purchase this place. I wonder what the asking price would be. In this economic climate, I would offer them half.' He bowed. 'Until tonight, Lady Hildreth.'

We shook hands and the chief and I began to walk back to the boat.

'What on earth is going on?' I asked.

'I can give you a full run-down on the prince,' he said. 'He asked for this meeting to be set up. Otherwise there is frankly not much to tell.'

'I don't believe that.' I pouted. Once again I wished he would put an arm around me.

He avoided my eyes. 'The questions we want answered are obvious,' he said. 'Why did the prince resign from the Saudi government? We think it may have something to do with a recent visit he made to the People's Republic of China. But it may be more to do with the rising tide of fundamentalism in his country. Our prince is a very glamorous Westernized playboy. Needless to say, we also need to understand the nature of his tie-up with Mr Assayd.'

'Your friend Sayff said they were enemies,' I ventured.

'Maybe' was my boss's only response.

We walked side by side for a few more steps. A workman on some scaffolding whistled from high above us. Suddenly, with a surge of courage which I could not have imagined mustering even a few days earlier, I linked my arm with his. I don't know what reaction I expected from him. I had acted on an impulse, a sudden, uncalculated abandonment of caution and reserve. I had not even considered his feelings. It was a unilateral move which left me slightly dizzy. I was conscious that I was beginning to lean on him for physical support. His response was to walk on as if nothing at all had taken place.

I remember noticing that a cruise ship with funnels shaped like the wings of a butterfly was steaming away from us towards the entrance of the harbour. Beyond the breakwater I was dimly aware of the swept-back lines of the chief's boat as it bobbed at anchor.

'Can we be off duty for two hours?' I asked.

'You're never off duty in this job,' he grunted. 'Mr Sayff is probably taking photos of us through his telephoto lens this very minute.'

I instantly withdrew my arm.

'Why didn't you say something?' I asked, deeply hurt.

'It would have been discourteous,' he answered simply.

'Is that all?'

For the first time in years I was allowing my emotions to govern my brain. It was probably all very stupid and hopeless. He had, after all, shown no direct tangible interest in me. No doubt all I was doing was working myself rapidly out of a very good job. In that case, I would simply have to find another one; or would I? The woman in me could feel his vibrations; at least, I thought I could. How real was his resistance? Perhaps he was shy, insecure, unused to dealing with this kind of situation. Was it being left to me to give a further lead, or did I run the risk of putting him off completely? Did he need time, or was it best to rush him? God, I wish I knew. It had become important, more important than anything else, than any other relationship I had ever had, including my marriage. I was confused. I wanted to fling myself around him and tell him how confused I was. Oh, these uncertainties. How they destroy human contact.

For the first time that afternoon, I felt the need to fill a vacuum in our conversation.

'This all feels a long way away from the Cots-wolds,' I said.

15

The wheels of the small British-built jet touched the sand-swept tarmac just after midnight local time. The large Arab opposite me stopped snoring and sat upright. We both peered out of the window at the four black limousines which were drawn up nose to tail on the runway beside us.

'You are being given the full treatment,' my companion commented. 'The prince will not be here himself but he has sent a high-powered reception committee. The man in white robes standing by the second car is Sheikh Khalif, the prince's private secretary.'

The pilot opened the aircraft's door and Mr Sayff led the way down the steps. A group of six men dressed in identical robes waited at the bottom. The man whom Sayff had identified as the private secretary stepped forward. He was surprisingly young and good-looking, beardless, with a black military-style moustache. He spoke quietly and, like Sayff himself, in perfect English.

'Lady Hildreth, you are very welcome to Jedda, both in your own right and as an esteemed representative of your government. His Highness is very much looking forward to meeting you. He realizes that it is getting late, but he hopes, nevertheless, you will feel able to have a first meeting with him tonight before retiring to bed.'

'That would suit me fine,' I pronounced in as formal a manner as I could.

He bowed and held out his arm in the direction of the second car. I moved towards it and the sheikh followed me.

So dark was it inside the car and so deep and far back the rear seat that I could hardly see the sheikh's face when he sat next to me.

'Your first visit to Saudi Arabia?' he asked.

I nodded.

'Then you will not have experienced the for you strange way in which women are treated here.'

'I was invited at short notice,' I said. 'I was not able to bring long dresses with me from France. Perhaps you would apologize for me in advance to the prince.'

He laughed. 'That will not be a problem, Lady Hildreth. The prince is very used to Western ways. He spends a good deal of his time out of the country. Nor will your dress be any problem inside the prince's compound. This is sealed off from the rest of Jedda. You will find life inside the compound very familiar. Even the swimming pools are mixed and the princess enjoys wearing swimwear in the most up-to-date Western styles. Nor, as I understand it, is there any reason why you should need to leave the compound. It would certainly be much safer for you if you did not. I can assure you that you are likely to find everything that you require inside the perimeter. We even have Western-style shops in there, not to mention three palaces, a school, a mosque, and even a radio station.'

There was very little traffic on the road as we drove into the centre of the city. Square sandstone houses began to loom on either side, shutters pulled down firmly over their windows. The street lights were weak and friendless and there was an eerie emptiness about the whole place. Two beggars sat wrapped in blankets at one street corner. Near them a policeman in khaki uniform, apparently oblivious to their misery, slouched against a lamp-post. Otherwise, I do not remember catching sight of a single human being. There were not even dogs about. At the far end of one street I glimpsed the reflection of the moon on the black waters of what I assumed was the Red Sea. At last the lead car in front of us made a sharp right turn and the short convoy came to a halt in front of a pair of large metal gates.

'We will have to wait here while the security guards check us out,' the sheikh said. They were the first words he had spoken for about ten minutes. Like me, he seemed to have been subdued by the bleakness of the place.

After a few minutes the gates swung open slowly. The view through could not have been more different from what we were leaving behind. Where up to now there had been sand and unlit blocks of houses, ahead of us there were floodlit lawns and luxuriant bushes. Beyond, I could see the colonnades of a large Grecian-style mansion. As we proceeded down a straight drive, I could just make out the outlines of other expensive-looking houses half-hidden by the shrubbery. Over to the right there was what looked like some sort of sports complex, with brightly lit tennis courts and swimming pools.

As we approached the front of the mansion, strong lights were blazing under the porch. The cars came to a halt in front of two vast glass doors. The moment we stopped, a tall gentleman in a red turban and military-style white uniform stepped out of the house. He opened my door and bowed.

'Welcome, your ladyship,' he intoned in an Indian accent. 'Please be gracious enough to follow me.'

He led our procession, as solemnly as if I were the Queen of England on a state visit, into a large empty marble hall. On the far side, two more Indian servants opened an ornately carved gilded wooden door. The room we now entered was more dimly lit than the hall. Its walls were draped in what looked like silk rugs. The floor too was covered in a variety of richly woven carpets. The furniture mainly comprised a set of about twenty gilded upright chairs dotted about the place in no apparent order.

In the middle of the room stood a man in his thirties. He was dressed in a dark suit, white shirt and blue tie. His height was about five feet ten. His shiny black hair was brushed with precision to the back of his head. His brown, slightly mocking, eyes were set in a face which I can only describe as pretty. To call it handsome would be to ascribe to it a ruggedness which it certainly did not have. He spoke, like his officials Sayff and Khalif, in aristocratic English.

'Good evening, Lady Hildreth. I hope you had a good journey. Will you take some refreshment? The only local produce I can offer you are some fresh dates. You may become rather tired of them by the time you leave this country. As for something to drink, in the compound there is everything, although I am sure you are aware that beyond the perimeter there is no alcohol. At least, there is meant to be no alcohol, though I am afraid you will discover that this is a land of rather widespread double standards., I have a ghastly feeling that the fundamentalists will sort that out one day. Now that's enough from me. Will you sit down, please?'

'Thank you, Your Highness. For the time being I will stick to orange juice, if I may, and I would certainly like to try some dates.'

'One Scotch and one orange juice,' he demanded of one of the Indian servants.

I sat down and the prince took a chair beside me. Sheikh Khalif positioned himself behind the prince, and the others, including Mr Sayff, retired to the far end of the room.

'As I invited you here,' the prince said, 'I think it is up to me, as they say, to open the batting. Incidentally, we must start a proper cricket team one day here in Saudi Arabia. It is a good game to watch and to play.' He took out a silver cigarette case and offered it to me. I shook my head and he said, 'I hope you don't mind if I do. It's a horrible habit which I picked up behind a bush at Harrow School. Despite being beaten for it twice, and quite rightly, too, I'm afraid I've never managed to throw off the habit.' A servant stepped out of the shadows to offer him a light. He puffed a ring of smoke towards the darkened ceiling.

'Now where shall I start? It is difficult. I will leave your friend Assayd until later. Let me begin with my resignation from the government. Contrary to the impression given in the Western press, I was never a very influential member of the administration here, although it is true that King Saud is my uncle. I was of some use in our negotiations with the Americans in the run-up to the Gulf War, but after that my Western connections were seen to be something of a liability. The influence of the Muslim fundamentalists has been rising very fast in this country over recent years, as you may know. Just how fast is really what my story is all about.'

He was handed a whisky and soda on a silver salver and he paused to take a sip.

'Exactly how far things have gone was brought home to me by accident. About three months ago, I was representing my country on a trade mission to

China. As part of this trip, I had to visit the city of Nanjing, which is on the Yangtze River between Beijing and Shanghai. I was met at the airport by the mayor of Nanjing, an old-style Communist Party boss. As we drove from the airport to my hotel in a car whose windows were curtained off, it became apparent that my host had been badly briefed on the purpose of my visit. He began to congratulate me on a deal by which, he said, my government was funding a massive rearmament programme in Syria. This involved the purchase of a substantial number of Chinese-made CSSI surface-to-surface missiles, each capable of propelling their warheads for more than six hundred miles. I knew about the missiles, of course, because we had ourselves previously purchased a quantity of them, despite the protests of our friends the Americans. What came as a very great shock to me was to learn that we were secretly helping to build up Syrian armed forces in precisely the same way as we had done, with such disastrous consequences, for Iraq. As you may imagine, I was especially outraged that as a member of the King's council I knew nothing about this. I have subsequently discovered that our funding of the Syrians has amounted to over five billion dollars since the Gulf War ended. I was so angry about this stupidity that I resigned my post as soon as I returned home. My uncle thinks he can buy off the fundamentalists in this way, but he is wrong. We have a saying that my enemy's enemy is my friend. In the same way, my enemy's friend should be seen as my enemy. Damascus is a friend of the potential insurgents here. It is a very dangerous course we are steering and I want your government, perhaps by using its influence with the Americans, to do what it can to reverse the policy, though I have to say I fear it may already be too late.' He withdrew a silk handkerchief from his breast pocket and wiped a bead of sweat from his cheek.

I was, to say the least, a little puzzled by what I had just heard and decided it was time to engage in the conversation.

'Surely, Your Highness,' I said, 'it would have been possible to convey these reservations and recommendations to our ambassador in Riyadh. Why, if I might ask, have you found it necessary to communicate through my department? This isn't quite our normal line of business, as you must know.'

He stared for a moment at the floor, apparently searching his mind for the appropriate answer. Then he looked up and turned himself in his chair to face me directly.

'I have told you only half the story,' he said. 'What I will say now will perhaps explain why I have contacted the British secret service. You may or may not know that I have certain investments in Australia. Part of this portfolio takes the form of shares in a large chemicals business in Western Australia, WA Chemicals. It is an impressive operation. I have visited it myself. The plant is very modern and the product range is well spread and successful. The profitability of the operation is in large measure due to the commercial cunning of our mutual acquaintance, Mr Assayd. Now I have to make a confession to you. Wherever I have large investments I try to introduce my personal representative into the business, to guard over my affairs; I suppose you might say to act as my spy. I have had such a person in place for several years with WA Chemicals. It is this gentleman who has reported to me on certain transactions which have occurred in recent months between Mr Assayd's company and the government of Syria, from where, it is my belief, Mr Assayd himself comes. To put it bluntly, Mr Assayd is exporting quantities of chemicals to Syria. I have reason to believe that at least two of the compounds are difluro and isopropyl alcohol amine. My advisers tell me that if these two are mixed together, the effect can be deadly. It would be nice to know what the Syrians intend to do with these substances, don't you think? If, for instance, they had developed the means to load them into the Chinese missiles, they would be in a position to wipe out my country.'

'Of course I now understand the reasons for your grave concerns, Your Highness. I suppose I am still mystified by why you chose to convey all this to me.'

'Because I knew that you were on Assayd's tail. I hoped at the very least we might compare notes.'

'I am genuinely surprised that you have this knowledge,' I said.

'Perhaps it would help to clear up your confusion

if I were to say that my representative in Western
Australia is Laurence Huntington, who is, I believe, a
cousin of a good friend of yours, the formidable Honourable Patricia Huntington.'

For the first time he smiled. I looked around me
and saw that the identical smile was implanted on the
lips of every one of his courtiers. Only the Indian
butler remained impassive.

16

Miss Fry, OBE, was, I thought, in a particularly protective and uninformative mood when I called in on her office the following evening. She sat stiffly behind her desk as I inquired whether the chief had returned.

'I wasn't aware that he had been away,' she said.

'Maybe I was misinformed,' I conceded hurriedly.

'Anyway, he's going to be in conference for the next hour or so. I have firm instructions to allow no interruptions until they have broken up.'

I knew Miss Fry too well not to ask her what was the subject matter of the conference. There was nothing for it but to retire to my own room along the passage and wait.

'Perhaps you would tell him that I'm back from Saudi Arabia when you have the opportunity. There is a matter of some importance on which I should brief him before he leaves tonight.'

'I will do my best,' was the non-committal reply.

As I unlocked the door to my office, my private telephone was ringing. I switched on the main light and walked over to my desk. When I lifted the receiver, a familiar voice said, 'Is that you, Jane?'

'Hello, Pat. Everything all right?'

'I'm fine, thank you,' she said, 'but there's something fishy going on outside your house. If I hadn't reached you this evening, I would have reported it in to the system.'

'Go on.'

'It's being staked out. Two gentlemen have been taking it in turns to sit outside it in a brand-new Ford Sierra.'

'How about going across and asking them what they want. That should frighten them off,' I suggested. 'Seriously, Pat, they must be amateurs if they are acting quite so openly. Either that or they want something from me. Pop over and have a chat with them and give me a ring back if you find out anything interesting.'

Ten minutes later, Pat was on the line again.

'You were right,' she said. 'They do want to speak to you.'

'What about?'

'They wouldn't say. They claimed it was highly confidential.'

'Did you say that I might not be back for weeks?'

'Of course.'

'How did they react?'

'They said that they knew for a certainty that you

had arrived back in the UK and that since it was now Friday, it was highly likely that you would be back home for the weekend. None of which I could reasonably deny because it's true. When do you expect to be down, incidentally?'

'Sometime tonight. I want to get in to see the chief before I leave if I can.'

The telephone went silent. 'Are you still there, Pat?' I asked.

'Yes.'

'Is something up?'

'The chief's obsessed about this Langhorn business,' Pat said.

'What makes you think that?'

'He's been twice on the scrambler phone to ask me what exactly it was that we discovered in Australia about John Harringay, Mrs Langhorn's brother. He's the one they say had an affair with the chief's mother, remember?'

'I remember very well,' I said and then added, 'Was that all?'

Her reply was non-committal. 'Let's just say that he seems much more wrapped up in this case than is normal for the head of the service.'

'You may have a point,' I said just as my internal phone rang.

'I'd better go, Pat. Someone wants me. I'll give you a ring before I leave.'

'What should I do about the Arab gentlemen?' she asked.

'You didn't say they were Arab. I'll cope with them when I get down, if they're still there.'

Miss Fry was on the other line.

'The chief will see you now.'

'I'll be right along.'

When I entered his office, he was sitting behind his desk.

'I've seen your report,' he said briskly. 'I wonder how much of all this the Israelis know. They've been ahead of us all the way down the line so far.'

'It is true, I suppose, that Her Majesty's Government's interest is marginal,' I suggested. 'One way forward might be to toss the whole thing at the Israelis and the Americans.'

His response was rather more emphatic than I had expected. 'Certainly not,' he said uncompromisingly. I reflected on the conversation I had just had with Pat Huntington. Perhaps the chief's preoccupation with this affair was becoming unhealthy. This feeling was not modified by his next remark.

'I'm not going to let this case go, not now. Assayd is clearly the key. Somehow we have got to get you back onto his boat. Did he give you an open invitation?'

'Yes, as a matter of fact he did, especially to his bedroom.'

If I had hoped this would dampen the chief's enthusiasm, I was disappointed.

'Think about it hard over the weekend,' he said. 'We've got to find a plausible reason for getting you back. It's the most economic way of discovering why the Studwell murders took place. It might also tell us whether Syria now has the means to deliver a warhead capable of killing thousands of people if lobbed at the right place.'

'As always, sir, I will do my very best.' As I rose to leave, I added, 'By the way, do you know who chose the swimwear you provided for me on the boat? Whoever it was not only had very good taste, but also knew my precise measurements.'

'I'm afraid I haven't a clue,' he said. 'As you know, I never get myself too tied up in the details.'

I was half-way through the door as I looked round at him with a mixture of frustration and fury. The fact that he was smiling simply made it worse.

I'm sure I forgot to say good night to Miss Fry as I rushed past her. I was still steaming with anger and humiliation when I turned right off the A441 and headed along the twisting road which leads down into Chipping Campden. A harvest moon lit up the rolling cornfields. In the distance, the lights of my home town flickered their welcome from the valley below. I sighed and began to calm down. The Cotswold hills invariably had this soothing effect on me. Anger turned to puzzlement. Why couldn't he just act like any other man? Why did he have to be so stuck up and difficult? Was it on purpose that he made things so hard? Or was that just the way he was? God, he was attractive.

I turned left in the town centre. To my right I

noticed that the car-park in front of the King's Arms was still full despite the late hour. As I approached my house, I saw the vehicle immediately. White and very visible, it was parked on the opposite side of the road, as it happened right outside Pat Huntington's cottage. Much to my surprise, as I drove up to the car, I found that it was deserted. I parked immediately behind it and knocked on Pat's door. When she emerged she was dressed, as was not unusual, in khaki overalls.

'Meet Hassan and Ali,' she said. At the moment of my entry the two young men were bending down, apparently to take the strain of lifting a car engine onto Pat's kitchen table.

'They're being terribly helpful,' she explained. 'This is the engine from the old Daimler I was telling you was giving me some trouble. That'll do very nicely, you two. Now come and meet Lady Hildreth and then we'll all have some coffee. If anyone wants it, I'm sure I can find something to eat.'

The taller of the two men approached me rather sheepishly. He wiped his hand on the back of his black jeans. We shook hands.

'My message is a very simple one,' he said. 'Mr Assayd asks me to say that if you agree to return to his boat, he will definitely do a deal.'

'I agree,' I said.

They left as soon as they had finished their coffee.

'Tell the chief that I have gone back as he requested,' I said to Pat. 'If I am not off the boat within five hours of my boarding, I am in trouble.'

'That will make him think,' she said.

'I doubt it,' I said. 'The man has a soul of iron. I don't think he possesses normal human senses.' I warmed to the theme. 'In fact, he's totally abnormal. He's what you might call a freak. When this job is done, I'm leaving. It's humiliating to be around him—I mean, such a crazy office.'

'Humiliating? After fourteen years?'

'The influence which he exerts over each one of us is unnatural. Someone has got to take a stand on it, Pat, and it looks as if it will have to be me.'

She leaned over the kitchen table and began to hammer at the piece of machinery lying in front of her.

Without looking up, she asked, 'This is all a bit sudden, isn't it, Jane? May one assume from it that you are falling in love?'

'I am going to have a bath,' I said and stumped towards the door. I paused with my fingers on the door handle. When I looked back, her smile was a lovely blend of amusement and sympathy. Since the death of my mother, she had become the only person in the world I really trusted.

17

From where I stood on the dock, the top of his bald head looked as if it had been burnt by the sun. Where it should have been tanned, it looked red. He gazed down on me from the height of the top deck. There was no wave of welcome. Once he was satisfied that I was boarding the ship, he turned away and disappeared from sight.

'I'll sort out your bag,' a voice called behind me.

'Thanks, Paul,' I called over my shoulder. 'Don't go to too much trouble. I don't intend to stay the night.'

He seemed surprised. 'I'll lock it in the skipper's cabin, then,' he said.

'There's not much in it. You can leave it on deck, if you wish. I can't imagine anyone will want to take it.'

'What time do you plan to leave?' he asked.

I looked at my watch.

'Let's see, it's just after eleven-thirty. I would have thought at about four o'clock.'

He scratched his head. 'That's very odd,' he muttered. 'Very odd indeed.'

A few hours later I was able to appreciate the significance of this short interchange.

When I reached the top deck, Mr Assayd seemed to be in a business-like mood.

'Let us sit down here in the shade,' he said.

As we walked across the scrubbed surface of the deck, the hot stillness of the morning was suddenly broken by two deep blasts immediately above us on the ship's whistle.

'You have been to Saudi Arabia,' he said as we took our seats.

'Your spies are as good as those of the prince,' I acknowledged.

'Perhaps because we use the same source.'

'Laurence Huntington?'

He inclined his head. I had been right. It was burnt and looked very uncomfortable.

'So you know of the biological and chemical materials. You know that Damascus has contracted for the means of delivery. What you do not know is how well advanced the whole package has become. Well, let me tell you. The whole thing is in place.'

'So what is there to discuss?' I asked.

'A reasonable question. If there were nothing to negotiate about, I would not have gone to the trouble that I have to invite you here again.'

As he spoke, the boat began to tremble. A high-pitched sound could be heard in the stern. I recognized this as coming from the winching system on the gangplank.

'What's going on?' I asked sharply.

'I thought you would like to cruise a little while we talked,' he said.

'As long as we don't go far. I plan to be off the boat by four o'clock at the latest. I have a plane to catch at six.'

'Have a drink,' he offered.

'No, thank you. Let's keep strictly to business for the time being, shall we?'

'As you wish.'

'Please lay out the terms as you see them for our discussion,' I said.

He took out a pipe from the side pocket of his cream-coloured jacket. I had not seen him smoke before. He knocked the bowl of the pipe on a table beside him. He began to fill it with tobacco from a pouch. In the distance, beyond the gunwales, the armada of moored yachts began to slip past us towards the stern. We began to increase speed as we swung towards the harbour entrance.

'We have everything in place except for one thing,' he said. He lit the pipe and began to suck hard on its stem. I said nothing, waiting for him to continue. 'We have the means to destroy Israel and even Saudi Arabia. What we lack is international acceptance for what we have done.'

'Poor you,' I said.

'You do not understand, Lady Hildreth. Unless

· 164 ·

this acceptance is forthcoming, we are bound to feel insecure, even threatened. And as long as that is the case, we are ourselves a threat to the peace of the Middle East. It will not be in a true sense our fault, but unlike that idiot Saddam Hussein, we will strike first if provoked.'

We were now passing the harbour-control office. A gentle breeze blew across the deck as we began further to pick up speed.

'Why are you telling all this to me?' I asked. 'I am an innocent employee of our intelligence services. This is all too grand for my department. Why don't you throw a lunch party for our ambassador in Damascus? Or, better still, take one of our young men in Brussels out for a cup of coffee in La Place de la Concorde?'

'Two reasons,' he said. 'First, because it was you who began to meddle in this affair when you visited Studwell Manor. You were first on the scene after we had decided to dispense with the services of Dr Swinton.' He added, it seemed in parentheses, 'Mrs Langhorn was pretty well on her last legs. We did little more than help the old lady on her way. We had, of course, had her under our control for years for reasons which may become apparent to you one day. The problem was that our means of control was weakening, and anyway, she had served her purpose.'

'And the second reason for choosing me as your go-between?'

'The second reason is that I like you, or, perhaps

more accurately, I have formed a deep attraction for you.'

I shifted uncomfortably in my seat.

He looked out towards the sea. The land was now fast disappearing in a haze behind us.

Then he turned to me. 'We are at sea,' he said. I was beginning to feel the rising tension between us.

'We are at sea,' he repeated, 'and we are alone.'

'What does that mean?' I asked.

'It means that I can make a proposition to you.'

I waited in silence.

'It is this: I am prepared to use my good offices with my government, and—I suspect you already know—my influence in Damascus is not to be under-estimated.' He took out a handkerchief from his trou-ser pocket and wiped the sweat from his forehead.

'I am prepared to persuade my government to enter into a pact with the Americans whereby we will agree to use the weapons we now possess only in self-defence. We would agree never to strike first against the Israelis.'

'And what must be done in return?'

'The Americans must agree not to attack us. That would be only fair. And you, my dear lady, must agree to become my friend.'

'And if I refuse?'

He leaned over to me and placed a hand on my knee. He stared directly at me. There was a look of triumph in his eyes.

'In that case,' he said quietly, 'we will find some

other way to make contact with the Americans and you will become my prisoner. In that event my requests will become commands, and you will obey my commands. You will do so because you will be my slave, my booty, the reward for my victory.' His eyes were bright with excitement.

'What is our present destination?' I asked calmly.

'A good question. You have clearly understood that we are not returning to Antibes. There is no harm in your knowing that we are sailing to visit some very close friends of my government, our brothers who rule Algeria. Their ideas run on very similar lines to our own. Now will you have lunch with me as an honoured guest, or must I ask you to submit yourself to arrest?'

'I have no problem in having lunch with you, Mr Assayd.'

'That is not quite the point, is it?' he rejoined. 'Lunch is a euphemism. In your country you have the expression, "There is no such thing as a free lunch." '

'In that case, perhaps arrest would be preferable.'

'You are being very foolish, Lady Hildreth. I do not wish our relationship to be founded on rape, but if that is the only option you give me . . .' He shrugged his shoulders.

'I cannot believe that that would win you many Brownie points in Damascus,' I said.

'I have told you that we might want to do a deal with the Americans, but we are by no means obsessive about it. I do not gamble, but on this occasion, I would be prepared to take a bet that any protests from the West about the way that I had treated you would be extremely short-lived. They would certainly not cut much ice back home in Syria. You Caucasians have no idea how much the people of the great states of the Middle East hate you. It is the one factor that keeps us all together. It is why Saudi Arabia armed the Iraqis and is now arming us, even though there is an appreciation there that we might one day cause the destruction of the ruling family. Now are you to be my friend or my plaything?'

I got up and walked over to the side of the boat. We were out of sight of land, and judging by the direction of the sun, heading due south. When I turned round, I discovered that we had been joined by someone who had presumably stepped out of a door beside the bridge. She must have been over six feet in height and weighed over two hundred pounds. She had long black hair which fell untidily down her back. Her skin was dirty brown and she had a thick nose like a boxer's.

'I will leave you in the company of Miss Hammed,' he said. 'You will now have time to come to your decision. I should advise you that Miss Hammed is well trained in most of the martial arts.' With that he walked slowly towards the stern and disappeared down a staircase at the end of the deck.

For her part, Miss Hammed seemed to take his departure as the signal to attack. Her lips curled and she began to scream in a strangely high-pitched voice.

'Face the wall of the bridge and put your hands above your head.'

I felt inside my denim shirt and withdrew my gun. She saw immediately what I was doing. She fell to the ground and crouched like a leopard ready to spring at me. I tossed the weapon at her feet.

The decision not to shoot her was a relatively easy one. I had absolutely no idea of the forces ranged against me. No doubt there were others like Miss Hammed in Assayd's entourage. It was inconceivable that she was operating on her own. Nor did I have sufficient intelligence about the professional crew. I had no idea whether or not they were personally loyal to Assayd. Paul Evans had seemed an innocent-enough fellow but I had no reason to believe that he would feel impelled to come to my assistance if I were to start shooting at his employer's friends. There was a time to fight, but this was not one of them. Instead I allowed her to push me roughly towards a door at the side of the deck. Inside the door we entered a narrow passage which led almost immediately to a lift. Miss Hammed towered above me as she pressed the call button. The lift must have been waiting on our deck because the doors slid open immediately.

We travelled five decks down to the depth of the ship. When the lift door opened, the air was hot and smelt of oil. The throb of the engine was oppressive, like the beat of a disco.

'This way.' She pushed me to the left. A few metres along a badly lit passage she turned a handle.

The cabin we entered contained two bunks, one above the other, and a wash-basin. Underneath it was a bucket. The floor space was sufficient to stand up on, as long as you were alone. There was no porthole.

'This is where you will wait until Mr Assayd has need of you,' she said. 'My advice to you is to make him happy. Mr Assayd is very generous to his friends. He is not so kind to his enemies.' Then she left. I heard the key turn on the other side of the door.

It was five hours before I had my first visitor. The woman who stood in the entrance to the cabin was much shorter than Miss Hammed.

'Good afternoon, Lady Hildreth,' she said politely. I had last seen her at Mrs Langhorn's cremation. I knew this by instinct, since on the previous occasion her head had been largely covered by a scarf. She was much more beautiful than I had taken her for on our first encounter. She had long black shiny hair and well-defined, sensual features.

'I tried to catch up with you after the cremation,' I said.

'I know.' Her laugh was faintly sinister.

'Why did you run away?' I asked.

'Why did I walk away, you mean? I left because my job was done. I had confirmed for myself by your presence at the funeral that the British intelligence service had a belated interest in Mrs Langhorn's death. That was all I needed to know. There was no point at all in hanging around for a cosy chat with you. You were of no further use to me.'

'It was you who murdered her,' I stated.

She shrugged. 'She had served her purpose. As a matter of fact, with your people and the Israelis hot on her trail, she was becoming a bit of a liability to us. As you have guessed, I returned to Studwell Manor for what you might call a definitive or final visit.'

'How did you do it?' I asked.

'It is not too hard with an old woman: one kick to the side of the face while she was sleeping. Then I rolled her body down the stairs to make it seem as though it had been an accident. Dr Swinton was more difficult. He had to be strangled and then transported to the chestnut tree. That was hard work, for which I required the services of an assistant who was also useful in drafting the fake suicide note. Did you know that Mrs Langhorn and Dr Swinton were lovers?'

'It was not necessary for me to know,' I bluffed.

'Even in her seventies she required sexual gratification. Imagine what she must have been like during the period of her so-called marriage. Without that, of course, things might have been very different.'

'Her marriage?'

'Yes. We knew every twist and turn of its falseness. That is how we were able to rule every movement she made.' Suddenly she paused. I wondered whether she had begun to feel that she had revealed too much to me. After a moment, she said, 'We must not be distracted by the past. It is the present which concerns us both. Mr Assayd, I assure you, is an excellent lover. It is important for you to know how he can be gratified. That is why I am here to advise you. I am, you might say, an expert on his appetites. I know what makes him happy.' Her large round black eyes were genuinely excited.

'I am unlikely to be a good pupil. Thank you all the same.'

She slapped my face with the back of her hand, on which I noticed there were two heavily jewelled rings. I could feel a trickle of blood roll down my right cheek.

She was smiling. 'I do hope that will not be necessary again, Jane. If we are to share Hisham, I want to be friends, or at least allies. I will return to fetch you in an hour or two. In the meantime, I am sure your training has prepared you to make yourself comfortable in your present circumstances.'

18

They came to fetch me at 10 P.M., almost eleven hours after I had first been imprisoned. This time I had two escorts; Miss Hammed was supported by the black-haired beauty. They had evidently decided to take no chances with me. I walked in between them with my wrists firmly handcuffed in front of me.

I expected to have to face Assayd when we entered the saloon on the main deck. As it turned out, the room was totally deserted, as indeed had been the passages along which we had walked to reach it. I had hoped to catch sight along the way of a familiar face among the crew; if not of Paul Evans, then at least perhaps of one of the two young stewardesses. But no one was about. It occurred to me that this was probably no coincidence, that they had been specifically ordered to stay out of my way.

We stood and waited. After ten minutes or so, I was allowed to sit down on an upright chair. Neither of my guards spoke. I had the feeling that they might have been as surprised by the delay as I was. At the end of a further half an hour the clock on the mantelpiece struck eleven. Two minutes later, to the visible relief of my two female guards, Assayd arrived.

The change in his appearance from when I had last seen him some twelve hours earlier was very noticeable. Gone was the cocky self-confidence. He looked tired and drawn. His skin was grey, his eyes slightly bloodshot. He crossed the room and seemed not to notice my presence. He slumped into a sofa and rubbed the palms of his hands against his face.

'Take those handcuffs off her,' he ordered. His voice was almost hesitant. With my arms loose I was able to turn more easily to face him and study him more carefully. He was clearly in some sort of trouble.

'You can leave us,' he said to my guards. Miss Hammed immediately rose to her full height. The girl who had claimed to be his mistress remained sitting.

'I thought you needed our help with this,' she said.

'I said go!' His voice had become more threatening.

She pouted and I thought for a moment she was going to defy him. Instead she too got up, flattened the creases from her short shiny gun-metal-coloured cocktail dress, and followed Miss Hammed out of the room.

'Now then, Jane, what shall we do?'

Extraordinarily enough, it sounded like a genuine question, as if he were really seeking my opinion. I decided that it was best to remain silent. This might further unnerve him. It might also force him to reveal what it was that was troubling him. It proved to be the right decision.

'Okay,' he conceded. 'If you won't talk, maybe I had better do so. The truth is I may need your help. You see, we have a problem on this ship. About an hour ago the captain received an unexpected signal. It was from the Jewish organization, Mossad. The message said simply that the ship had been mined with devices which were timed to go off in about an hour from now. When they do they will totally destroy the boat and, needless to say, all those still on her.'

'So what action have you taken during the past hour?' I asked.

'We have searched the ship, but with no luck.'

'Do you have a bomb-disposal expert on board?'

'An amateur one. You have met her: Miss Hammed can set and defuse most established devices.'

'Why then has she been wasting her time sitting around here with me?'

'We haven't told her what's going on yet.'

'Why not, for heaven's sake?'

'Because the captain decided that until we had found the devices we should keep the information restricted to himself, to me, and to one member of the crew. He did not, in particular, want panic to set in, especially amongst the temporary staff, such as the stewardesses. They have been advised to get some sleep in preparation for a busy day tomorrow.'

'So one hour has been wasted and there is only one more to go. What do you plan to do now?'

'To seek your help,' he said wearily.

'Does the captain know that you have had me locked up for the last twelve hours?' I asked.

'No.'

'Who does?'

'Only the two girls.'

'Lucky no member of the crew saw me being brought up here earlier on.'

'It was a mistake to put you in handcuffs. I agree that would immediately have alerted any member of the crew who saw you that there was a problem. We would have had to tell them that you had been found stealing company documents from my briefcase and were being kept in custody until we handed you over to the authorities in Algeria. But it is true I might have had to face some hard questioning from the captain. It would have been difficult. He would have asked to see you.' He shrugged his shoulders. 'One plays these things by ear. As you know, I would have much preferred to have had you as a friend. I became obsessed with the fantasy of possessing you. The less you wanted me, the more excited I became by the prospect of overpowering you. I confess I was encouraged down this path by the two ladies who have just left. Miss Hammed was especially excited at the prospect of aiding and abetting in your humiliation and submission. I'm afraid she's a dangerous woman, Miss Hammed.'

'So you've tried finding the bombs,' I said. 'How can you be sure that this is not a hoax?'

'My people in Damascus have been in touch with Tel Aviv. It is not a hoax, unless the Israeli government are lying, and I cannot think of any reason why they would wish to do that.'

'Equally,' I said, 'it is difficult to see what they have to gain by blowing up your ship.'

'Revenge,' he said, 'an eye for an eye and a tooth for a tooth. We Arabs understand that. We have much in common with the Jews in so many ways. I think that is why we hate each other so much. We know each other too well. We have each risen up out of the desert over thousands of years. Had it been the other way round, had it been the Jews who had developed a sophisticated biological weapon of the type we now have, I would have wished to have revenge on the person who was responsible, even though I would know, in the sense in which the phrase is used in the West, that it would do no good. They cannot make us disinvent what we have created, but they can try to destroy the inventor. I neither blame them for that nor do I accuse them of being crazy.'

I stood up. 'This is not getting us very far,' I said, 'and a further five minutes have passed by. What is to be your next move? If what you are saying is true, there is not much time left.'

'I wish you to contact your office,' he said slowly. 'There is an American aircraft carrier in the area. At the very least, they would have the helicopters to winch off the people on board before the ship blows up. It's possible also that if they commandeered the ship, the Israelis might be able to defuse or delay the bomb by remote control, though my impression is that they have left themselves no flexibility on that score. If your office were to request the help of the Americans, they would be bound to respond positively.'

'I would need to take complete control of the ship,' I said at once, 'and you and your friends would be required to surrender unconditionally to me. The captain will be fully informed of what is happening and about your situation. Before I make any approach to London, I would also require the return of my weapon.'

He stared at the wall ahead of him. 'I understand,' he said without looking in my direction.

'Let's get on with it then,' I ordered.

Five minutes later I was on the darkened bridge alone with the captain. He offered me a cigarette, which I refused.

Then he said, 'What a bastard. If only I had known what was going on. My God, I would have laid into him with my bare hands. I've got a good mind to launch the dinghy, put the crew in it, and leave him to blow up. The problem is that there is quite a high sea running and it's pitch-black out there. There isn't even much of a moon tonight. It would be very hazardous. Of course, if the Yanks won't help within the next half hour or so, we may have no choice.'

'Just leave me with the ship's radio for a few minutes, will you, Captain, and I'll see what I can do. I would like to do this on my own. Get Paul Evans to keep an eye on Assayd and his women.'

'Do you know how to work these things?' he asked.

I nodded. 'I assume it's standard equipment.'

A few moments later, I could make out the familiar voice. My hand suddenly began to tremble as I heard him laugh.

'I was expecting you,' he said.

'What?'

'When I didn't hear from you, I assumed something must be up. We tried to reach you by radio but were told that you had asked not to be disturbed. That didn't sound at all plausible.'

'Now what's going to happen?' I asked.

The response was drowned in a heavy burst of static.

'I can't hear you,' I shouted.

His voice returned in faint waves of sound.

'Are you alone?' he inquired.

'Yes.'

'On the bridge?'

'That's correct.'

'You are using the main transmission system?'

'I cannot be sure of that. There may well be other connecting devices. It's possible we are being monitored.'

'I have no option but to take that risk.' Once

more his voice became inaudible. I thought I caught the word 'contingency' but I could not be sure even of this. Then suddenly he broke through loud and clear.

'You should know that we have the Israeli bombs under control.'

The door to the bridge crashed open behind me. The captain stood facing me with a gun pointed to my head.

'Take off the earphones!' he shouted.

'I've got trouble, Chief,' I said and allowed the mouthpiece to fall to the deck.

'You were, of course, correct in assuming we were following your conversation,' the captain sneered. 'With the Israeli threat "under control," to use your boss's own words, we will now reach Algeria in comfort. Nobody is going to blow this ship while you're on it.'

19

The captain stood aside as Mr Assayd emerged on the bridge. He removed a pair of reading glasses which I had not seen him wear before.

'This is all very sad,' he said. 'It would have been much better had we managed to develop a sound relationship with the British intelligence service. I must share in the blame, of course. I became a little unbalanced in my attraction for you, Lady Hildreth. I suppose I had hoped that the feeling might be mutual and I was angry and hurt when I found out that it was not. I freely admit I over-reacted. Now, of course, it is different. Now we are at war with each other. Please consider yourself to be a prisoner of war. As such you will be treated under the conventions applicable to an enemy agent captured in civilian clothes. I hope one day we will be able to bring you to trial as a spy. In the meantime you will be summarily shot if you make any attempt to escape. In that case I cannot even promise that your body will be returned to your next of kin.'

He turned to the captain and was on the point, I think, of giving him instructions as to how I should be dealt with, when the door behind him opened. Paul Evans emerged from the darkness outside. His face was flushed and he looked angry.

'What the hell's going on?' he demanded. The man at the wheel, who was the fifth person on the bridge, coughed. 'Why has the on-board lighting system been switched off? Did you order it, James?' Paul demanded of the captain.

I watched his superior's reaction with interest. He stared without blinking at his second in command. It occurred to me that the captain's high cheek-bones, sallow skin and wiry black hair did not quite match his Anglo-Saxon name.

'Yes,' he replied coldly.

'What the hell for?' Paul seemed suddenly to notice the other three occupants of the room. 'What's going on here?' he asked.

'There's been a change of plan, Paul,' Mr Assayd said. He had retreated to the darkened rear of the bridge.

'What I think Mr Assayd is saying is that you and I and any other member of the crew who is not part of his gang are in a spot of bother,' I ventured.

'Stand where you are,' the voice said from the shadows.

When he stepped into the dimly lit centre of the bridge, Mr Assayd was pointing a gun at Paul Evans's stomach. At that moment the ship's radio began to ring. The captain turned towards me. He too was now armed.

'Maintain the present course,' he said to the man at the wheel. 'I'll deal with the radio.'

The rest of us stood in silence while he picked up the receiver and listened to the incoming voice. He gripped his gun in his right hand while he held the ear-piece in his left. He made no attempt to respond to whatever message he was receiving. After a few seconds he replaced the earphones on a hook above my head.

'We are surrounded by American warships,' he said.

Mr Assayd said, 'It would seem, Omar, as if Allah the Great has called us to our moment of destiny earlier than you or I had anticipated. Are you able to speak with the Americans?'

The captain replied in Arabic, which I understood well enough to be able to make out that he had been supplied with a contact number.

'Go to it then,' Assayd commanded.

The captain punched several numbers into the keyboard of the radio set. After a moment, he said, 'My name is Omar Alirud. I am captain of the *Pacific Queen*. I am sailing under the flag of Syria. I have on board a senior representative of the Syrian government. We demand safe passage to Algerian waters.'

I could not hear the response but it did not seem to be entirely favourable. The captain frowned.

'I will discuss this with my principals,' he said.

He replaced the head-set and waved his gun at me. 'Go across and remain beside Evans,' he said. 'There are insufficient seats, so you will sit on the deck.'

As I moved across the bridge, he began to talk heatedly in Arabic with Assayd. After a few minutes he returned to the radio. This time there was a note of urgency in his voice.

'We insist,' he said, 'on safe passage. If this is refused, we will destroy the vessel and everybody on it will perish. I hope I have made myself clear.'

I looked up at the windows overlooking the bow. Somewhere in the pitch-black night outside several warships must be closing in on us.

'Contact Hammed and Ishmar,' Assayd said. 'Tell them to come up to the bridge.'

When they arrived, the two ladies seemed to be slightly out of breath.

'You will be responsible for guarding these two,' Assayd said. 'There is also the question of the stewardesses. They must be secured. The rest of the crew is reliable. They were recruited personally recently by Captain Alirud.'

Miss Hammed screamed at me, 'Lie on your front. You as well, Evans. Place your arms behind your backs.'

For the second time that day, I felt the cold grip of the handcuffs snap around my wrists. A blindfold was tied tightly around my head.

'We will sail a direct course,' I heard the captain say. 'I will ask Mussafet to arrange the explosives.'

'Once you are satisfied that all is in order, we will ask Lady Hildreth to act as an independent witness to the fact that the ship has been turned into a potential fireball,' Assayd said. 'She will inspect the explosives so that she can relay the facts of the situation to her friends. In this way we may save her life, at least for the time being.'

The bridge went quiet. At one point I heard the door to the deck outside bang shut. I must have lain in this way for about half an hour. Then, suddenly, I felt the top of a boot in my back.

'Get up!' Miss Hammed ordered. Slightly disorientated by my blindfold, I rose shakily to my feet.

'This way.' I was dragged by my right arm in what I presumed was the direction of the door to the bridge. Outside on the deck it was a relief to breathe in the cool sea air. I stumbled and fell as the boat rolled.

Someone pulled me back to my feet. Then we were in the lift. When we came out, we turned left. The noise of the engines was becoming deafening. We must have been almost on top of them. I could smell their fumes. The heat was beginning to make me sweat.

Someone said, 'Remove the blindfold.'

Assayd stood in front of me. He was uncomfortably close. I could sense Miss Hammed's presence behind me.

'Look to your right,' Assayd ordered.

I did as he requested. I knew enough about explosives from my days fighting the IRA to appreciate that the system wired up to the outer casing of each of the two engines was either an elaborate hoax or, if live and activated, would undoubtedly completely destroy a vessel of the size and characteristics of the *Pacific Queen*.

'Please feel free to take a closer look,' Assayd suggested. Without actually dismantling the system, I had seen enough.

'I am prepared to believe that you are ready to blow up the ship,' I said.

'That is all I need to hear,' he said. 'Now I want you to transmit that information to your office in London.'

'The government I represent doesn't trade in hostages,' I said.

'I am no longer interested in your views on this matter,' he said. 'We will return to the bridge.'

When we returned to the bridge, the room was in almost total darkness. The captain was leaning over the radar screen, his face illuminated in eerie green.

'Three ships closing in to port, two to starboard, and one to our stern,' he reported.

'Call that number,' Assayd ordered.

'Very good.'

A minute later the captain shouted over to Assayd, 'They are ready to receive your message.'

Assayd crossed over to the radio set.

'Dr Assayd speaking,' he said. 'I think you know of me. I wish you to speak to the British agent, Jane Hildreth.'

Miss Hammed pushed me across the room. The earphones were placed over my ears.

'I am speaking to you under instruction from my captors,' I said.

'Very good, ma'am,' an American voice responded. 'We read you loud and clear. What is your message?'

'You are to say that you have seen that the ship is wired for destruction.' Assayd stood beside me. His hand gripped my arm.

'I am told to say that the ship is wired up with explosives.' I felt the jab of a gun in my back. 'I have been shown some equipment which lends support to this,' I added.

'You are speaking to us from the bridge of the ship, is that correct, ma'am?'

'Yes,' I said readily. It was a firm part of our training to try to answer questioning from friendly parties in circumstances such as these as directly as possible.

'May we speak next with the captain?'

I handed over the equipment. I heard Alirud say, 'Yes, I am aware of the ships in the area. I repeat that any hostile act will be met with the instant destruction of my vessel.'

At that moment there was a deafening bang. The whole bridge suddenly exploded into light. Instinctively I looked towards the door, where there was now a gaping hole. I fell to the ground as the first stun gun found its mark with the captain. The next to fall was the helmsman and with him Assayd. Miss Hammed screamed. The other woman drew her gun. There was a slight thud and she fell forward. Suddenly the room seemed to be filled with figures in wet suits.

A voice said, 'Take over the controls.' Another shouted my name.

'Over here,' I called back, 'and the bloke lying in a heap in the far corner is a friend.'

20

Pat Huntington surveyed the red-brown polished surface of her Chippendale dining-table. When I ate with her, we usually did so in the kitchen. It was exceptional for her to have laid out her heavy silver and beautifully cut crystal glass in the dining-room. In my memory it had happened only once before, when she had been trying to match me up with what turned out to be a very unsuitable Texan billionaire.

Through the latticed windows I could just see the elegant Georgian shape of my own house across the road. The wisteria climbing up the front was just coming into full bloom. The lilac and the honey-coloured stone blended in perfect harmony. A little girl in a blue-and-white-checked dress and with two little red-haired pigtails suddenly emerged from the shadows made by the setting sun and roller-skated shakily past the windows of my drawing-room. The large ancient pavement flagstones eventually proved too much for her and she toppled backwards onto her bottom just before she went out of my sight.

Pat looked at her watch.

'Seven o'clock. He should be here in about half an hour. He's driving over from Banbury.'

'Is that where he lives?'

'Close by.'

I didn't embarrass her with further questions.

'He's been very elusive for the last few days; indeed, ever since you got back.'

'He's never been easy about the Langhorn affair,' I said.

'I know. It has all been too close to home.'

Then, as if wanting to change the subject, she said, 'Let me get you a Campari and soda, or would you like something a little stronger?'

We carried the drinks into her little drawing-room. I was struck once again by the beauty of its contents. Not for the first time, I wondered whether she had bought any of the pieces herself, or if they were all inherited: the Georgian glass corner cupboard with the exquisitely hand-painted china, the Queen Anne sofa table, the walnut knee-hole desks, the Jacobean mirrors, the Elizabethan portraits? Had she taken time off in the past from mending cars and maintaining her skills as a marksman to collect beautiful objects? I knew her so well. She was my closest friend. There would be no one to replace her, and yet she retained her mystery. It was part of what made her so unique. Now it was I who looked at my watch.

'Don't worry,' she said, 'he'll turn up. He was pretty enthusiastic when I invited him over.'

'What reason did you give?'

'I told him that I would not live forever and that he would regret it if he had never visited my cottage before I died.' Then she winked. 'I said nothing of the kind. I simply told him that you and I were planning to have a quiet supper together and would love it if he would join us. He said yes before I had finished the sentence.'

'You didn't have to argue him into it?'

'Hardly.'

'The last time we met it wasn't easy,' I said.

A car came to a halt in the road outside. We both sat up.

'I'll go,' she said.

'Wait till he presses the bell first.'

'You're acting like a schoolgirl,' she said. 'It's perfectly charming.'

When he came into the room he was wearing a dark-blue blazer and well-pressed grey flannel trousers. His white shirt was open at the collar. Under it he wore an orange-and-gold-striped silk cravat. He carried a bunch of red roses and handed them to Pat.

'You said it was very casual. I hope you meant it,' he said.

'You look very nice,' Pat replied.

He turned to me. 'Welcome home,' he said.

'Thanks for sending such a fine body of men to rescue me,' I replied.

'The Special Boat Service hasn't lost its touch, has it? They don't talk about themselves as much as the SAS seem to do these days, but they're pretty effective for jobs like that one.'

'What have you done with Assayd?' I asked.

'Put him on a plane back to Syria. There was nothing else we could do. We will probably have to give his ship back in the end. Our political masters are not in a mood to fall out with the Syrians, however much we may warn them about their new military potential. It was the same with Iraq, and before that with Iran. They believe, wrongly in my view, that it's all a question of playing them off against each other. The problem with that is that it ends up with the whole region turning itself into a particularly nasty arsenal of nuclear, biological, and God-knows-what arms. I suppose someone will listen the day that one of the big European capital cities is within range of one of their missiles. Judging by what the Chinese and the North Koreans are now coming up with, that should not be far off. All very disturbing, don't you think? May I have a drink, Pat?'

'What sort?' Pat asked.

'Gin and tonic, if you've got one.'

'How very depressing,' I said. 'It's a story without an end.'

'Not altogether. For me it has at least exposed the mystery of the Langhorns. It's something that has bothered me for most of my life. You know that my mother had an affair with John Harringay?'

'Yes.'

'There was something about the whole business which never did quite tie up. Now I know.'

'Let's hear about it over supper,' Pat intervened. 'I've roasted a pheasant. It always used to be your favourite.'

'It still is,' he said. It was as if he were a small schoolboy home for the holidays. For a moment I had to remind myself that he was head of the nation's counter-intelligence services. Placing an arm behind my back, he guided me into the dining-room.

We sat opposite each other, a single candle flickering in a silver holder between us.

I began to toy with the smoked salmon in front of me. He unrolled his napkin and stared into the flame of the candle, its light giving a phantom-like pallor to his face. Suddenly I felt very nervous.

From the end of the table, Pat said, 'Have a glass of wine, you two. Would you mind pouring it out, Adam?'

Neither of us seemed to hear her. I can only speak for myself, but I had moved into a new and strange level of existence. Everything seemed to go very still. I wanted to reach out and touch him but somehow felt unable to move or to speak. It was as if I were taking part in a film whose projector had broken down. I was stuck in a single motionless room.

I heard Pat speak again. 'Why don't you finish the story about the Langhorns?'

At this he seemed to jolt back into motion.

Colour returned to his cheeks. To this day, I remember his every next trivial movement as if it were of momentous importance. He lowered his right hand towards the table and simultaneously turned his head towards Pat. He picked up his fork and then, as if making a decision of some significance, replaced it. A slight tremor vibrated through the surface of the table. Then there was a tightening of his narrow, slightly receding jaw as he spoke.

'Ah, yes.' He paused. This hesitancy was very unlike him.

'Go on, dear boy,' Pat encouraged.

'It certainly provides some justification, I suppose, for why my mother should have tried to have a close relationship with John Harringay. At least in the eyes of the public, and I suppose of the Lord, he was a free man. His only real love seems to have been for his sister; Mother could, I suppose, have argued that that didn't count. What I'm leading up to, my dears, is that John Harringay and Mr Langhorn were one and the same person, though that development, of course, came after Mother had died.'

The room fell silent once more. Pat was the first to speak again.

'Strange that I failed to recognize him in the pictures we found. He must have changed in looks a good deal over the years, because what you are saying is that Mr and Mrs Langhorn were brother and sister.'

'That is, of course, another way of putting it,' he

conceded, 'and for many years there was only one man in the world who knew their secret.'

'Cousin Mick,' Pat suggested.

'How did you guess?' he asked.

'The intuition of a good agent,' she answered stiffly.

'Veronica Harringay confessed to him. Knowing he was besotted with her, she assumed he would keep the secret, especially as it may have been part of an arrangement whereby she would one day become Mick's wife. These hopes were dashed, of course, when John Langhorn, as he called himself after the war, died and Veronica failed to return home to Australia.'

At this point I felt my balance sufficiently restored to be able to join in the conversation.

'This explains the likeness between the two of them that we noticed in the photo of the beach scene.'

Then it was Pat's turn to intervene. Her face glowed in the candle-light and she stated, 'You said, Adam, that Mick kept the secret for many years. That implied that eventually he let it out.'

'That is correct. When Veronica failed to come back to him after John's death, he became very saddened, not to say probably a little bitter. He and his cousin Laurence started to go out on heavy drinking bouts together. It must have been on one of these occasions—I think in response to some accusation by Laurence that he was homosexual—that Mick blurted out the truth about the Langhorns—stroke—Harringays. Needless to say, he deeply regretted what he had done the next morning. But by then it was too late. Laurence had the ammunition he needed to launch a vicious campaign of blackmail. At first all he wanted from Veronica was money, but later he teamed up with Assayd, and we now know the consequences of that.'

'Tell us precisely,' I said quietly.

'With your intelligence, dear Jane, I'm sure you will have worked out most of it for yourself. Mr and Mrs Langhorn were controlled by the permanent threat hanging over them that their incestuous relationship and false marriage would be exposed. They were forced by Laurence and his clients to exploit their entrepreneurial skills and their very considerable knowledge and experience of chemicals to develop increasingly nasty substances which could be used for aggressive military purposes.'

'My cousin Laurence is quite a boy,' Pat broke in. 'He was also on the payroll of Assayd's enemy, Prince El-Mummed.'

'Oh, yes,' my boss conceded. 'He is on everybody's side so long as the pay is right. I imagine he thought, with some prescience, as it has turned out, that he had better hedge his bets against the Syrian job coming to an end one day. I doubt whether it will be too long now before one of Laurence's clients decides enough is enough and slides a knife in his back. I'm sorry, Pat, but having known him most of my life, I won't shed too many tears for him.'

'Let's hear the end of the story,' I said.

'There's not much more to tell. After Mr Langhorn's death, a high-powered chemist called Swinton was sent to team up with Mrs Langhorn. As you know, he became her lover. Then the time arrived when they were both dispensable; more than that, their continued existence became a positive threat to the success of the Syrian venture. I'm afraid this was in part due to the fact that both Mossad and ourselves were beginning to take a close interest in what was going on at Studwell.'

'By which time it was all a bit late,' I stated.

The light of the candle flickered over his distinguished features. His eyes were lowered towards the table. The thin line of his mouth hardly moved as he said, 'You can't win them all.'

'One last question,' I requested, 'then we can change the subject. What did you make of the photographs with the headless bodies we found amongst Mrs Langhorn's effects?'

He turned towards Pat. 'One of those bodies was yours, my dear. Remember that time when Aunty Veronica visited us just after the war? In the picture she had her arms around Mick Huntington. No wonder she didn't want her brother, husband—call him what you will—to recognize everyone when she brought the photo back to England.'

'So the figure of the small boy must have been yours, Adam.'

'Yes,' he said flatly.

Pat scraped back her chair. She rose from the table and went over to the window. The light outside had completely faded. Silently she pulled the curtains.

It was not until she had returned to her place that she said, 'I remember how miserable you were at the time. It was just before you were due to leave for boarding-school in England. However, it's worked out in the end, hasn't it, dear? I'm so glad I've lived long enough to see it all. Your mother would have been very proud.' She paused for a moment and he made no attempt to fill the vacuum. When she spoke again, her words sounded distant and remote. She looked tired. 'She would have liked you to have had a family. The trouble is that you have been so busy. I know that better than anyone else in the world. Too busy for a long-lasting relationship. I suppose the truth is that we've both been busy. In my case I haven't stopped for fifty years. I imagine there'll be more time to think where I shall be going soon.'

I felt the tears swelling in my eyes. I looked across the table at her. For the first time that evening, I stared straight into his eyes. This time they made no attempt to avoid me. I stretched my arm across the table towards him. He took hold of the back of my hand and squeezed it. Then he turned to Pat and asked, 'Do you think I might invite her to stay at the farm?'

· 198 ·

Pat smiled as only she could. 'I'm not her mother. She can speak for herself.'

'Mrs Chadwick can act as chaperone,' he added hurriedly.

'How boring,' I said.

The echo of our laughter drifted up into the beams of the old house and so back into the mystery of time.